BLACKLIGHT CHRONICLES
BOOK ONE

FIRE
MAGE

JOHN FORRESTER

AMBER MUSE

ISBN-10: 0984825916

ISBN-13: 978-0-9848259-1-2

Cover Design by Anca Gabriela Marginean

Visit: www.blacklightchronicles.com

To my loving wife and two wonderful boys,

for all your support and patience.

1

The Hunt

Talis searched the steamy swamplands for prey, hoping to make his father proud, no matter what the cost. For some reason his father's words echoed in his mind, *"Your brother hunted big game when he was twelve."* Why did his words etch in his mind like ink on a page? His brother had hunted with a team of men and merely managed to bounce his spear off a deer. Talis was thirteen now and though he'd tried, had been spurned by every hunting trip his father's men had pursued. *Lad, don't want you dying like your brother, you're the last son of the Storm family lineage, and all.*

Finding nothing all day, he scanned the muddy ground for tracks, kicking away needles and sticks. Off to the corner of his eye he spotted an indentation in the wet leaves. He strode over and bent down, flipping his hair away from his eyes for a better look. A thrill raced through him at the sight of fresh tracks. He raised his head and studied a sloshing stream blanketed with a soft mist, and squinted at a path illuminated by the four moon sisters. This was his kill.

"Did you find something?" said Mara, his best friend. She wore sage-green hunting pants and a ridiculously frilly white lace top, why, he had no idea. She was funny like that. As she came alongside, she raised her big brown eyes in concern, and glanced at the tracks. She chewed a cinnamon stick and frowned.

He grunted in response and pointed a short spear with a menacing, curved blade at the stream. This was his hunt and even though he'd failed to even bag anything as big as a deer, he swore he'd do anything to bring it back home to father.

Mara shook her head, the movement stubborn and terse, her short, brown hair slashing along her neck. "It's too late. I'm serious, don't look at me with those oh-please-Mara eyes of yours."

"But the prints are fresh, an hour old at the most."

"What are you trying to prove? We've been out here all day and my ass is sore from sliding down that stupid muddy hill. I'm hungry, irritable, and want nothing more than to eat a slice of peach cobbler, steal a mug of ale, and prop my feet up and feel the heat of the fire. Besides, I'm not going to let you get yourself killed doing something stupid as hell like hunting in the dark."

"Don't be angry." He flashed her the look he knew always made her smile, and gazed into her devilish, incredibly-cute amber eyes, hoping to convince her. But it didn't work this time. She set her jaw firm and scowled at him. He tried a different approach and lowered his voice until it was as soft as a cat's purr. "Listen, we can do it...can't we try just one more time?"

"It's your father, isn't it? You think he's going to instantly respect you if you bring back something big? He doesn't really see you the way you deserve to be seen. Ever since your brother died..."

The wind stung from a sudden cold gust and Talis sighed, wishing she hadn't brought up the subject of his older brother's death. He cursed fate, cursed his family's bad luck, and memories flooded his mind of his older brother Xhan. His arrogant, youthful expression. A cruel death in the desert.

"You know I'd hunt with you to the Underworld and back, I really would. We're a team. I just hate seeing you go on and on like this. Can't we try another night?"

"Please...it would be amazing if we succeeded. We can do it, we've planned this hunt for months." And in his mind he pictured tossing the slain creature at his father's feet knowing he'd achieved something Xhan had never dared.

A blur of movement ahead in the bushes caused his attention to jerk up in a quick second. He stopped and searched around trying to spot the source. There, beyond a patch of Elderberry, something fat and filthy waddled down a muddy path. His heart pounded and jumped at the sight. This was it.

Tensing his muscles, he bent low, stalking after the animal. He glanced at Mara, and sent her a victorious grin. It was a big, burly boar. He followed after the tromping creative until it reached the stream and grunted at a wallow surrounded by a circle of mossy rocks, finally settling into the mud. This was his first chance at hunting a boar. But when he really got a good look at the fat beast a jolt of fear shot through him. *Those are some massive tusks*, he thought.

But by now Mara had already nocked an arrow. Their plan all along had been to weaken the boar at range and switch to spears and daggers to stop its advance. Seemed like a bloody stupid plan now staring at the powerful creature. Part of the plan always included dragging the boar back to Mother's kitchen for a fine roast. And seeing Father's proud eyes as he said, *"You're a fine hunter, son."* An unlikely dream.

At Mara's questioning look he quickly nocked an arrow and nodded at her. She turned back to face the boar, but her eyes remained wary and fearful. This would be a tricky shot. He leaned to the side and felt the tension strain his arms as he pulled the string back, aimed, and released the arrow straight at the boar. It was a good shot, but the arrow caught a thicket's branch and droned off past the creature. Damned! How could he miss?

The boar jerked its head up and glared at Talis. He barely had a second to think before the beast sloshed in the stream, bounding towards him. He ducked as Mara's arrow flew past him and slammed into the boar's chest. Why was he just stupidly standing instead of nocking another arrow? Another shot from Mara hit the boar's flank, and she fired off another one that hit the creature in the hip. But the arrows didn't seem to slow the boar down at all.

Eyes mesmerized at the advancing boar, he shook his head and threw down his bow and quickly brandished his spear. Mara did the same and spread out in a circle as the boar aimed directly at him.

He jutted out his weapon, ready to strike, but again felt fear latch onto his heart and squeeze until he found himself gulping deep breaths through his mouth. Mara shouted for him to watch out.

As the boar's tusk bore down on him, Talis leapt out of the way just in time and thrust his spear down at the beast. The creature squealed in pain as his spear pierced the back of its neck. Mara lunged at the boar with her spear and stabbed its rear flank. It shrieked, swung its tusks around and knocked her back onto a pile of leaves.

Talis screamed as he watched her spin through the air and slam backwards onto the ground. A sickening feeling twisted in his stomach. What had he done? Fury raged in his chest and he stabbed and prodded the boar, trying to keep it away from Mara, until finally the creature gave up and bounded away, howling and grunting in a mad rush.

Gods, why didn't I listen to her? He ran over to find Mara wincing, her eyes vacant and bloodshot, but still conscious. She tried to lift herself up.

"Wait, don't get up. Rest a moment. " Talis tried to remember exactly where the tusk had struck her. "Where does it hurt? Wait, don't close your eyes! Look at me, are you all right?"

She coughed and inhaled a huge gulp of air and coughed again, a redness sweeping over her face. "It knocked my breath out...there are stars everywhere!" She started to laugh but crimped up in pain. After ten heartbeats she began to breathe normally, and pushed herself up with the help of Talis. But when she tried walking, she stumbled and leaned on him for support.

"You're seriously hurt!"

"I don't feel so great." An agonizing grimace gripped her face. "I probably need help getting home."

He had to get her back. And quickly. Why the hell hadn't he listened to her?

She wobbled, then slapped her palms to her stomach as if she wanted to vomit. Talis seized her just as she was about to topple to her knees. A shiver went through her body as she tried to steady herself. She winced and wiped a hand across her mouth. A line of blood sat menacingly on her wrist. She gaped at her hand.

Now he was beyond worried, and knew he had act quick or she might not be able to make it.

"I think I'm going to be sick." Her face went pale as she looked at him with frightened eyes.

Talis lifted her into his arms. "I'm taking you home. Now." He thanked the gods she was so much smaller than him.

He carried her, stumbling down the bluff, ignoring her protests. A wound like that was incredibly dangerous. If he didn't get her to a healer soon, he knew Mara might die. If anything happened to her he knew he'd never forgive himself.

After a long while he was too tired to carry her, so he rested for a bit, his breath heaving and stiff arms and legs protesting. Even though it was almost dark, Talis could see that Mara's face looked white as chalk. He had to keep going, no matter what, no matter how much his legs and back burned from carrying her.

By the time he spotted the City of Naru from afar, moonlight sent long, wiry shadows across the hillside leading up to the towering stone walls. He told himself he could do it. No matter how hard it was to keep carrying her, in his mind he was determined to keep her alive.

Lights flickered from countless braziers mounted hundreds of feet higher on the upper part of the city.

Naru stood ominous under the garish light of the four moon sisters, and as the evening gong sounded from atop a watchtower, Talis knew he had made it....

He stumbled towards the main gates, barely able to stand anymore, and a group of soldiers making their rounds noticed and ran over to help.

"Young Master Talis, what's wrong?" said Baratis, the captain of the guard, and his eyes blazed fear at sight of Mara. "Is she alive?"

"I can't talk now...open the gates...she's hurt!"

"Carem and Jorem! Help them," Baratis shouted.

The two soldiers lifted Mara from Talis's arms and carried her through the gate. Massive steel shafts stared down at them from inside the stone walls as they jogged past. If they weren't quick about it, she would die. Talis ran ahead, urging them faster. Eyes blinked at them from behind murder holes as they entered. Archers ready to strike down enemies in a siege.

Spread before them past the gate was the Arena of the Sej Elders, formed of gigantic white granite blocks, rising over everything in the lower part of the city. Stone towers lined the wide avenue leading up to the arena. They had to move faster.

The soldiers' boots clapped against the cobblestone streets as they marched past the arena, finally winding around until they reached the gates to the upper city.

Up the snaking rise, they charged past merchant shops and eyes that gawked at the soldiers carrying Mara. They continued on, to the highest part of the city, beneath the Temple of the Goddess Nestria, the Goddess of the Sky. To Mara's house, the House of Viceroy Lei and Lady Malvia, daughter of the king and second in line to the throne.

They were going to be furious, Talis knew he was in serious trouble for taking Mara out on the hunt. But he couldn't think about any of that, all that mattered now was Mara's life.

As the soldiers carried Mara into the white marble mansion, Talis worried that her wounds were too grave to cure. Today was the worst day, and he was all to blame. Why did he have to chase after the boar? Two servants ran up and gasped when they noticed Mara, and they quickly helped her inside.

Lady Malvia rushed towards them, her silver robe swirling behind. "What has happened to my daughter? She's so pale, can someone tell me why she's so pale?"

"A boar…we were out hunting—"

"Gods, Talis!" She brought her hands to her face, an expression of horror paling her eyes. "Boar hunting? You're both only thirteen! What were you thinking?" Her face seethed with concern and rage. "I

13

warned you two about hunting alone. Now go and fetch the healer! Go!"

A sick feeling wrenched his stomach as he raced out back to a small, mud-thatched building overlooking the rose garden. It was his fault. He never should have insisted on going hunting in the first place. He vowed not to go on the hunt again—not if it meant hurting Mara.

Inside the healer's apothecary, he found Belesia grinding herbs inside a gnarled, wooden bowl. The room held the pungent smells of mold, fire and smoke. The walls were lined with jars of herbs, roots, dried insects and small, shriveled animals floating in clear liquid. The healer narrowed her eyes at him.

"Young master…what brings you here?"

"Quick, you have to come now. Mara was injured in the swamp…by a boar."

Belesia clasped her hands over her stomach. "Wait. First tell me, is she bleeding?"

"From the mouth." The vivid image of blood dribbling from Mara's delicate mouth wrenched Talis's heart.

She groaned. "How did it strike her?"

"Tusks slashed here." He pointed at his lower ribs. "And later blood spilled from her mouth."

"An internal wound, this is a grave injury…" She rummaged through several herb jars and grabbed various roots and mushrooms and stuffed everything inside a satchel and hobbled outside. "We must hurry."

As they made their way through the mansion, Talis's heart pounded and his palms went flush with sweat. Mara was going to be all right, wasn't she? Belesia came from far to the west, lands renowned for their magical healing powers. But this kind of injury was different and Talis was unsure if it was curable. The thought terrified him.

Inside Mara's room, she lay in bed, feverish and flushed. Death stirred in her crazed eyes. A servant swabbed a wet cloth on her forehead, crying uselessly, a look of horror and panic on her face. Belesia rushed to Mara's side and pressed her palms over her forehead and stomach.

"The wound is deep…the flow of energy blocked. The fever, rising."

Belesia chanted words from a strange tongue, words sharp and shrill, words from the western islands, lands filled with the magic of the earth and the spirits. Her eyes narrowed to small slits, and the room dimmed and prickled with electricity as her chants grew louder.

In the darkness, the healer's hands glowed red like burning embers and Mara's body filled with light, as if her veins pulsed with iridescent gold. Mara's eyes flung open, unseeing, as if she stared at something that only existed far away in her mind. Was she seeing the guardians of the Underworld coming to summon her spirit? Talis stepped forward to hold her hand, to bring her back, to keep her spirit here, but Belesia motioned him away.

"Will she be all right?" Talis whispered, his voice choked and terrified.

Belesia raised a finger. "Her wound lies in her internal organs. My power is strong, but the healing will take time to regenerate the organs. And I'm sorry to say, m'lady, sometimes the healing fails...."

"Fails?" Lady Malvia said, her face turning pale as ash. "But you will do everything, won't you? I can pay any amount, grant you titles and lands, but save my daughter!"

The old healer cackled softly and muttered words to herself as she gazed at the faces of ghastly demons circling over Mara's bed. "When it comes to magic and the gods, money means nothing. Pray to the gods, dear lady. You and your entire house. And you, young master Talis, pray most fervently as well. Pray to Tolexia, the God of Healing."

"I will…I promise. I'll do anything, gods willing, to keep Mara alive." Talis bowed his head and pinched his eyes shut, saying the words of prayer to Tolexia: *God of Healing, God of Harmony, listen to this mortal's plea for Mara. Fair Tolexia hear my prayer and save her life, with my heart pure and mind full of penitence.*

When Talis opened his eyes, Lady Malvia stared at him with a mixture of disappointment and fury. Talis withered at her glare and found himself retreating from the room.

"I want you out of this house." Lady Malvia's voice was as sharp as an executioner's axe. "If she lives you'll save your family from shame and bloodshed. For only blood will satisfy blood. And the gods may ask for your blood if Mara dies. I allowed Mara to hunt with you on the condition that you'd protect her, and now you bring her home like this? You always had the option to take the rangers with you." *But the rangers always laughed at me and refused to join,* Talis wanted to say.

She motioned with her eyes for a servant, and the man led Talis out of the mansion, his calloused hands rough on Talis's arm. Please let Mara live, please, Tolexia, please. He kept seeing Mara's shining face, laughing and teasing him. She was his best friend. He'd ruined everything today by his foolishness, and put Mara's life in danger. Her life was worth more to him than all the hunts in the world.

He stumbled down the cobblestone street, bumping into carts and people, barely able to see straight with the tears blurring his sight. It was only a short way to his house, the House of Garen Storm, but he went the wrong way down towards the shops and the marketplace, and had to turn around and trudge back home. Somehow he reached his mansion and a servant ran inside to alert his parents. He lowered his shoulders and sighed. How could he face father now, after all that had happened today?

She would live, the gods were good, she would live. He willed it so. Talis felt the truth burning in his heart.

2

A Feather for a Friend

Garen Storm came limping down the dark hallway,
carrying his hawk-headed cane as if it were a weapon.
Talis cringed at the dark expression on his father's face
as he swept aside his silk cape, black eyes glaring at
Talis, and he puffed on a pipe, sending smoke swirls
rising into the gloomy air. The candlelight from the
servant standing on the side of the room sent flickering
dark gashes across Father's face. Why was Father lately
always so dark and serious?

"What's your excuse this time?" he muttered,
tapping the cane against his hairy hand. "Haldish,
bring some light in here, I can barely see a thing."

"Yes, Master Storm." Haldish bowed and set the
candle on a long wooden table containing several
carved statues of the gods. Talis stared at the beautiful,
ivory statue of the Goddess Tolexia, the god of healing,
and made another silent prayer for Mara's recovery.

"We were out hunting…Mara was hurt by a boar."
Talis glanced at his father's raging eyes, but quickly

looked away. His father exhaled angrily and muttered curses, then Talis heard him hobbling towards the fire at the hearth in the great room. At least he didn't hit him with his cane, though how Talis felt now, he almost wished that he did.

"As if we don't already have enough trouble with House Lei." Father sat at a plump, leather chair in front of the fire. "Now you force me to make amends with Lady Malvia...if she'll see me. Is Mara hurt badly? Go on...sit...this is not an execution."

Talis obeyed, feeling the leather chair warmed by the fire. Part of him wished Father was harsher, he felt guilty, he felt what he did was wrong, but he just sighed and nodded gravely. "She's bleeding internally from a boar's strike."

"Blood awful..." Father ran his fingers through his thick, black mane. "Has the healer treated her? Should I summon healers from the Order of the Dawn?"

"Belesia has cast her magic...and Mara sleeps. I've prayed to Tolexia." *And even now I feel the power of the Goddess surrounding Mara, wrapping her in light.*

"May the gods favor her recovery. I'll go visit the Shrine of Tolexia tomorrow and pay House Lei a visit." Father frowned, disapproval spilling from his eyes. "I know you and Mara have been hunting for years, but you're too reckless, boy... Boar hunting?

You could have both been killed. Once again you disappoint me."

Talis felt himself shrink back at Father's words. This would all have been different if they'd managed to bring back a boar to Mother's kitchen. He noticed his mother leaning against a marble column, staring sadly at him. Talis nodded and she waved back.

Garen glanced at his wife. "All that I'm saying is…be cautious, be more like your older brother…" His voice faltered and broke, and his eyes reddened suddenly. He closed his eyes as if remembering his son, and after awhile raised his clenched fists towards the sky, his face puffed and fuming.

"Why, Nyx? Why did you have to take Xhan away from me?" He pushed himself to his feet, faltered a moment as if dizzy, then he turned and tromped off, retreating once again into his study, the place where he often locked himself away from the family, in the years after Talis's older brother Xhan had been poisoned during a battle with desert marauders.

Mother crept forward and put her arms around Talis. She hugged him for a time, and Talis could feel the worry and blame melt away from his mind.

"You can believe she'll be all right. Have faith in the gods. Let's get you some food." Mother led him into the kitchen where his younger sister, Lia, played with her favorite white doll. "Why don't you rest with your sister, she's been worried about you."

"Why was I so stupid?" His voice cracked and he placed his hands over his head. He felt somehow that *he* was to blame for the way Father acted since Xhan's death. Father was right, if he was more careful, Mara would never have been injured by the boar. His mother sat next to him and he told her what had happened in the swamplands.

Lia squeezed his hand. "Mara will be all right...I just know it." His sister was so delicate and feminine, and her eyes held certainty and innocence, with a wisdom beyond her seven years.

"Darling," his mother said to Lia. "We should make an offering at the Shrine of Tolexia tomorrow for Mara."

She nodded, her face beaming, and she glanced concerned eyes at Talis.

"Can you eat something? Or perhaps some soup," his mother said.

Talis shook his head. "I couldn't eat a thing...my stomach feels sick."

"Then go to bed... There's nothing you can do right now, except perhaps beg favor from the gods."

He bowed his head, and once again prayed to Tolexia for Mara to return to health. He turned and shambled outside and up the stairs to his bedroom loft. Before going inside, he gripped the rail and stared out over the city of Naru, lit with the pale light of the four moon sisters. Thoughts of Mara and Lady Malvia and Father raced through his mind. And Xhan, his older brother, why couldn't he even picture his face anymore? Did the power of death do that to memories? If Mara died, would he forget her face as well?

After several days of worrying about Mara's condition, with no reports from Father or Mother, and Lady Malvia's refusal to allow him access to see Mara, Talis thought of a way to find out how she was doing. That afternoon he slunk behind a tree near the side gate to Mara's mansion, waiting for the healer, Belesia. She usually ran errands in town around this time, and around twilight, the wooden door creaked open, and Belesia stepped out onto the cobblestone street. She wrapped her shawl over her shoulders and strode down towards town. Talis followed her from a distance, past the royal mansions, past the merchant's houses, past the upper markets and their sweet smells of bread and cakes and ale, until they reached the dingy lower part of the city.

All Talis could think about along the way was whether Mara was all right. Would Belesia be under orders forbidding her to tell him anything? But he couldn't believe that, the healer always did what she wanted, valuing the gods and friendship more than anything else. She was a friend, wasn't she?

When they entered Fiskar's market, Belesia stopped at a stall where a man with a twenty-pound tumor in his neck sold mushrooms. Belesia haggled with the man for a long while, clucking disapprovingly at the price, then finally handed him a few coins and clutched the bag under her arm and left.

Talis seized the opportunity and jogged up to her. Belesia turned her head, as if knowing he was there. "I'm surprised you didn't follow me sooner."

"I tried to respect the wishes of House Lei." He didn't want to get in more trouble than he already was.

"People say things they don't mean when they are angry." Belesia took his hands. Her skin felt warm and leathery. "Your friend is close to recovery."

"She is?" Talis couldn't stop the smile from spreading across his face. He felt the tension go out of his shoulders, as if he'd released a heavy pack. "And is Lady Malvia still upset at me?"

Belesia rubbed her hands together. "Time heals foolish actions...and your father knows the right words

24

to sooth Lady Malvia's fire. You may not know it, but they were once close friends like you and Mara. That is until Lady Malvia decided to marry your father's old enemy, Viceroy Lei."

Father and Lady Malvia? "I didn't know…Father talks little of the past, save for talk of Xhan."

With that, Belesia came close and placed a hand on Talis's cheek. "The living sometimes suffer more than the dead. Give your father tenderness. His heart still bleeds."

She turned and strolled away, her words still lingering in his heart. Talis pictured Father's face after the news of Xhan's death had reached him. He had suffered and Talis realized he hadn't been there to comfort his father when he needed it. Maybe there *was* more he could do.

A laughing couple tramped by and the girl bumped into Talis. She bowed her head in apology and giggled as they strode off. Talis glanced around at the merchant stalls, thinking of Mara again, and decided he should find a gift for her. A gift to make her eyes sparkle.

The air in Fiskar's Market smelled of roasted venison, pork, chicken, and sweet pies from the baker's oven. He sauntered around, scanning the vendors hawking their goods: sacred charms, shrunken heads, colorful jewelry studded with precious stones, Orbs of the Sun and Eyes of Death, and prayer beads sold by gold-toothed monks. Greed in their eyes. Why did monks seem more interested in coin than in meditation to the gods? Fiskar was long dead, but the name stuck. He was smart enough to set up business and sell in front of Shade's Gate and next to the Temple of Nyx, the God of War.

Talis discovered a merchant who claimed to have recently purchased amber feathers with white flecks, plucked from a rare bird found along the Southern coast of Galhedrin. Whenever he pictured the southern seas he imagined adventure and sultry nights, swordplay and pirate ships ravaging towns along rocky shores. How he longed to explore beyond Naru. But Talis knew this was impossible, he was too young to ever be allowed in Father's trading caravans. Especially after Xhan's death.

Yes, a feather would be a perfect gift. Mara was crazy about collecting feathers. She loved to adorn her hunting hats with immaculate feathers from all over the world. But these were new, he'd never seen such brilliant feathers. So he bought a particularly beautiful feather for her using money saved from pelts he'd sold from hunting in the swamplands. A small fortune.

Out of the corner of his eye he spotted Nikulo, a boy he knew from the Order of the Dawn, where they both studied magic. Nikulo learned the healing arts. Didn't he worship the Goddess Tolexia? Talis thought of Mara's injury. Perhaps Nikulo could help him win favor from the Goddess. Not that Nikulo was likely to help him. Talis focused on elemental magic at the Order of the Dawn, although his success was limited to magic done in training dreams. And lately those had always turned into nightmares. The eyes of Nyx, the moans of the Underworld, his brother's face suffering. Talis had never managed to produce magic like the other apprentices and felt very frustrated at his many failed attempts.

Nikulo scanned stalls off in the back corner of the market, and stopped to buy something from a merchant Talis was sure sold poison and other black arts supplies. As if afraid of being seen, Nikulo glanced around several times, frowned, and marched towards the stall where Talis stood.

Talis tried to hide behind a bunch of feathers, but Nikulo stopped, and glared at him.

"Cowering already? You know you don't have a chance of winning the Blood Dagger."

The Blood Dagger competition. Talis thought of the sparring competition held once a year, and froze, realizing he'd forgotten all about it. Wasn't it only a few days away? With Mara injured, they'd moved the date, but Talis knew that House Lei and House Storm would never allow Talis and Mara to forfeit to the likes of Nikulo and Rikar, his sparring partner. Claiming rights to holding the Blood Dagger for a year meant far too much to the royal houses, especially since their house had lost claim to the victor's rights over the last few years.

Nikulo's coffee-brown eyes sparkled as if he was eager to tell a new joke. He waddled close to Talis, holding a porcelain jar in one hand, and he yanked up silk pants that kept falling below his protruding belly. He scratched his curly hair and released a smoky fart, blowing the fumes in Talis's direction. Talis coughed, retreating quickly. Nikulo never should have swallowed that last potion he concocted. All his farts smelled like sulfur and spoiled onions.

"Thanks for that, just what I needed." Talis rubbed his stinging eyes. "What are you doing slumming in Fiskar's Market? Finding more noxious ingredients for your potions?"

Nikulo moved the jar away from Talis. "No...nothing of the sort." He frowned, and pursed his lips. "Why are you holding a feather?"

"It's for Mara. Why are you hiding that jar?" Talis gave Nikulo a determined scowl.

"Oh this?" Nikulo glanced around at the jar he was holding. "Just ingredients." He fidgeted, constantly glancing at Shade's Gate, the way to the upper part of the Naru where Nikulo lived.

"Ingredients? What for? Weren't you at the poison merchant?"

"Poison?" Nikulo coughed out an offended laugh. "Why would I want anything to do with poison? You know it's not allowed for students of the Order." Nikulo narrowed his eyes, studying him for a time, as if trying to decide if he could trust him or not. He cleared his throat and went on. "When is Mara supposed to get better? Rikar and I are getting tired of waiting to fight you guys. If you don't compete soon, the Blood Dagger will be ours."

"You know that's not going to happen. You'll taste our blades soon enough. Are you so anxious to have your blood spilled? Mara will be better soon enough, just you see."

Nikulo chuckled. "You're lucky that House Lei hasn't sent an assassin after you."

Talis waved his hand as if the idea was ridiculous. "I've got to go. Be careful with that poison… Another failed alchemy experiment and you're likely to kill someone." But then again, maybe that was Nikulo's idea, poison merchant after all... Maybe he was working on something to give him favor at the Blood Dagger competition. Again Talis imagined his brother Xhan dying of poison, and grimaced, finding his hands clutched over his stomach.

The next morning Talis awoke in a fright to spot spindly shadows dancing across the room as the wind knocked the shutters back and forth. He hated waking this way. His cat, the yellow and white Tobias, pounced on his bed, tail jerking crazily, staring above at the amber feather he'd bought for Mara. It flipped around in the breeze, taunting Tobias torturously.

Talis had mounted the feather on a strand of leather tied to a wooden beam that spanned across the ceiling. The cat leapt into the air, trying to swat the feather, but missed it by a few inches.

"You little devil." Talis tried to scoop up Tobias, but the cat darted about the room as if possessed by a ghost. "You can't have Mara's feather, it's not your toy to play with... I'll get you a duck feather or something. Come on now."

The shutters suddenly slammed opened and Talis spun around. Mara was perched on the windowsill, grinning viciously at him. Mara was here? And she looked all recovered.

"Miss me?" She jumped inside the room and dove into his bed, then wriggled under the covers. Her hands were uncomfortably near his pants. Talis felt his face flush from the surprise of seeing her here. Tobias pounced onto the bed, leaping high into the air every time Mara moved her hands under the covers, deliberately teasing the cat. Tobias meowed, a complaining meow, and the cat stared, as if trying to figure out what was going on.

"You're all better?" Talis went to hug her, then realized she was lying in his bed and he felt his cheeks go red in embarrassment. Mara raised an eyebrow and lowered her voice to a whisper.

"Way to state the obvious. No"—she coughed and clenched her stomach, rolling over in bed—"I'm about to keel over and die." She laughed maniacally and pulled the blanket over her head.

"Be serious, I thought you really might die. We were all so worried! I prayed so many times to Tolexia…"

"You can't kill a cat that easily. Though you sure did try!"

"Me?"

"Just kidding!" She stretched her arms wide and wiggled her body towards him. "Somebody here is so in love with me. I bet you couldn't stop thinking about me, right?" She stopped and glanced up at the feather. "Is that for me?"

Talis nodded, then jumped up to grab the feather.

Mara squealed when he handed it to her. "It's gorgeous! I bet it cost a small fortune... Didn't it? It'll look great in my green hunting cap. I can't wait to wear it."

He smiled, and braced himself as she jumped and flung herself onto him, giving him an enormous suffocating hug. She stayed there for a long, uncomfortable time and he could feel her soft breath on his neck. She whispered *thank you* in his ear, and slid down his body to stare up at him. From the look of beaming happiness on her face, it was worth every silver piece buying her the feather.

She motioned towards the window. "Why aren't you offering to take me to breakfast? Can't you see I'm hungry?"

"Whatever you want, it's my treat, thank the gods you're better." He sighed and fixing his eyes on her, nodded. "It's really good to see you, Mara."

A blush appeared on her face, but she quickly snorted as if to avoid embarrassment. "If you want to know, I'm craving dumpling soup from Fiskar's Market. Hurry up, already." She pulled her hood over her head and scrambled out the window.

3

A Demon's Eyes

Usually royals believed that going down to shop or eat in the lower part of the city was far beneath their station. That's why Talis and Mara almost always went there, to escape prying eyes. Especially now, since if they were seen together, it would mean trouble for both of them. As they strolled down the freshly-washed cobblestone street, Mara whispered to Talis that her mother was still furious at him and they had to be careful.

Mara ran ahead, as if trying to put distance between them. He wished they didn't have to skulk around and disguise themselves or face the wrath of Lady Malvia. They always took the trader's way to Fiskar's Market. Around the upper shops, down an alleyway stacked with crates, inside a warehouse door, past workers loading crates, until they reached the dark warehouse room that led to a corridor winding around down to a lift.

The workers always averted their eyes from them when they used the lift, as if they thought it wasn't their business to notice a few royal children stalking around in the building. Talis and Mara hopped on the lift, and she grabbed his hand as the lift jolted, starting their descent several hundred feet down in the darkness.

Talis always felt a thrill on the descent, as if uncertain whether they would ever arrive at the bottom. It was pitch black without a source of light. Mara cuddled close to Talis, her arms snaking around his waist, the soft exhalations of her breath landing on his neck until he felt uncomfortable and his heart raced. Her small fingers felt along his chest and she wormed her way even closer and started to whisper something in his ear.

The lift suddenly jolted as they reached the bottom. What was she going to say? She jumped out of the lift and dashed down the passageway until they reached Shade's Gate, next to the upper part of Fiskar's Market. Talis frowned and wondered if he ever would understand the minds of girls.

Today was Hanare, the sacred day of the Goddess Nacrea, eighth day of the week, a day free from study and work. At least for the royals. In Fiskar's Market, most commoners still toiled, preparing for Magare, the first day of the week and market day. But still, children chased chickens lazily through the market stalls and old men played Chano, staring at the chipped granite pieces as if waiting for a mystery to unfold.

Old women gossiped, casting curious eyes at Talis and Mara as they sat at a flimsy table next to a boiling pot of pork dumpling soup. The broth smelled of garlic and chives and roasted hare. His stomach grumbled.

Talis handed the cook two copper coins. The man wiped his dirty apron and stared suspiciously at the coins. He grunted and filled a ladle full of cabbage, bits of meat, shimmering dumplings, and piping-hot clear broth, slopping the soup into a blue ceramic bowl. Talis salivated as the man placed the bowl in front of Mara, and glanced at the man with expectant eyes.

"Can I start?" she said, dumping so much chili sauce in her soup it turned red.

"Torture me…"

She slurped the soup and made a face of pure joy. "This tastes so amazing! I wish our cook could make soup as good as this. I'm so sick of the strange food they've been giving me."

"Can I have a dumpling?" Why was the cook taking so long for his soup?

"Yours is coming soon enough. So impatient!" She winked at him with a flirtatious grin on her face.

The cook scowled at Talis, as if contemplating whether he should server him or not. Finally, with grudging eyes, he slopped the soup into a smaller bowl (skimpy on the dumplings and meat) and plopped it down in front of Talis. What was wrong with him?

"I've got news for you." Mara held up her spoon like a professor giving a lecture.

Talis slurped the soup, wincing at how hot it was. He grunted for her to continue.

"Mother wants me to marry Baron Delar's son—"

What the hell? Talis spewed the soup onto the ground and coughed. Him? Baron Delar's son was twenty-eight, how in the name of Nyx could she marry him? It was ridiculous!

"The soup is hot, you should be more careful." Mara smirked at the look of horror that must have been on his face. "Don't you approve of the engagement?"

How could anyone approve? But Talis wasn't going to give her the satisfaction of being jealous. "I don't know…I guess it's good news. Congratulations?"

"You idiot! Are you kidding me?" Mara's eyes raged with righteous vexation. "I'm not marrying that pig-faced, smelly old warthog. He wears frilly silk blouses. Why would a man dress like a pampered child?"

"But all the lands he owns, and the trading routes, titles..." Talis forced himself to look serious, despite laughing on the inside.

"I can't believe you actually think it's a good idea," she shouted, drawing in stares from the cook and many others nearby. He grinned at her finally.

"Settle down," he said, softening his voice like he was speaking to a baby. "I never said it's a good idea. Eat your soup, will you? You can't be married until you're fifteen anyway."

"What's so funny? Stop chuckling at me." Her eyes flared in fury. "It's two years away! Besides, engaged is as good as being married...it's like a prison. Nobody breaks their engagement—well there was Lady Macela—poor thing, and she never got married. Isn't she all on her own now? But to that old pig? What are my parents thinking? I truly despise them."

"Just tell them you don't want to marry him."

"I already did. You know they never listen to me. They claim they know what's best for me. I'd rather run away than marry him. I simply won't do it." She cast a venomous glare at her soup, then sighed and looked up at Talis, raising a finger as if she had an idea.

"Let's win the Blood Dagger competition. If we win, we're allowed any wish we choose. That'll keep me away from that ridiculous man."

"But Rikar and Nikulo are undefeated…and they're brutal—"

"I don't care! We can do it, I know we can. Ever since that old witch made me drink all her potions and tea I feel strangely powerful…like I can do anything."

"We've had a string of bad luck, though. We lost two times in a row in the training arena. And then you almost got killed by the boar." Talis lowered his voice to a whisper. "It's like the gods are angry with us."

"There are rites of initiation we could try…a blood oath."

"A blood oath?" Talis swallowed, not liking whatever was implied by her suggestion. "Would that be with the Temple of Nestria or Nyx?"

Mara glanced at the vines covering the walls surrounding the Temple of Nyx, the God of War. Talis followed her gaze and felt a chill prickling along the back of his neck. "I know what we have to do. We must pray to Zagros, who favors the weak and fallen."

Zagros? What insanity would cause them to pray to the God of the Underworld? "I don't know if that's such a good idea…"

"Listen, we know the rites of initiation. We've been trained, right? What are you afraid of?" At her determined gaze Talis felt a clammy coldness creep down his spine. This was a terrible idea.

"The Temple of Zagros is for those bringing the dead...or those who worship dark magic. We've learned the rites in case someone in our family dies, and to ensure their swift passage to the Fair Seas. But why would we go there now?"

"I'm not marrying Baron Delar's son. We've prayed to the other gods before previous matches and we still lost. What have we got to lose?"

Talis believed that they'd be risking everything, even risking losing their own souls. "Oh let's see, I can think of many reasons why it's a bad idea. Demons. Curses. Necromancery. And just purely summoning the wrong kind of attention!"

"You owe me." Mara said each word slowly as she fumed, her face red now in rage. "I won't allow myself to be sold off like that. Besides, it's not like it's the first time in history people have performed the rites in situations like ours. We both read the words and we were trained by the same priests. All those with royal blood have a tie with the God of the Underworld. It's our privilege—"

"And our cautionary warning," Talis interrupted.

She went on, ignoring his words. "Many heroes in the past have done the rites of initiation to ward off death's touch. We'd be doing it for victory and a powerful god's blessing."

Glancing at the twisted black oaks marking the entrance to the Temple of Nyx, Talis frowned, knowing this was a horrific idea. But after five heartbeats of staring into Mara's pleading eyes, he gave in, realizing he would do anything she wanted. She withdrew a small silver knife and pricked her thumb. Blood dribbled out. Talis gave her his hand and winced as she did the same with his thumb.

Her eyes wild with zealous determination, they leaned in close to each other and pressed their bleeding thumbs together, whispering a sacred vow to complete the Rites of Zagros. Now they could do nothing but follow through until it was done. Although as to what consequences this would bring, Talis had no doubt that they were dire. Even stretching beyond the grave.

Talis stood, appetite obliterated, and together they stepped hesitantly towards the blackened iron gate of the foul-tempered God of War. The all-powerful, ever-wrathful Nyx. Once inside the temple grounds, the air seemed to darken, either obscured by the oaks or frightened by the shadowy crows that cawed and cackled in the quavering branches above. Talis forced himself past, despite feeling lead weighing down his every step. Mara tugged on his hand, and led him around the sword-shaped temple of forged iron, and past the onyx gravestones that marked fallen war veterans. Generations and generations of generals and heroes and soldiers of noble birth slain in the defense of Naru.

Closer to a wall of tangled and twisted vines, Talis found the air reeked of sulfur and festering mold. Mara covered her mouth in disgust, then coughed and puffed out her chest, eyes intense, and faced the wall. She chanted words of passage to gain access to the temple grounds of Zagros.

"For there were four winds racing from the four corners of the world, four spirits and four demons, consuming all life in their path. Grant access to your dominion, yet hold your devouring fire till old age."

With those words spoken, the choke vines moved, loosening and untwisting, and shaped a small shadowy path before them. Talis had a sudden desire to flee, to run back to the safety of the marketplace. Eyes locked with Mara's, he clenched his jaw and stepped towards the opening. They squeezed their way inside where a wild, warding power surged in the air, the power of protective dark magic, the power of the barrier between life and death.

The sky collapsed to a whorl of gray and black as tiny scintillating bolts formed an electric mesh in the sky. A barren ledge stood before them. Beyond, the vast Nalgoran Desert stretched across the horizon, desolate and filled with dust devils traversing the sands. The sky seemed to fall down and embrace the desert, merging into a reddish-brown being. The wind rushed at their faces as they strode up to the ledge, the ledge where many chose to plummet to an early death. *The Devil's Grace.*

Talis stepped gingerly towards the edge, mindful of the lack of railing, and wished he'd never agreed to perform the Rites, but said the words of entry, "All powerful Zagros, finish the deed, grind all matter to dust, from the remains the seed springs to life."

He stared out over the vast expanse to the east with nothing but sand and whirling wind for hundreds of miles. He felt something out there waiting for him, calling him, a craving stirring in his legs.

Mara tugged at his hand, pulling him to the left towards a cave set inside the massive granite cliff.

"Are you sure this is a good idea?" he whispered.

She frowned. "You vowed. Just whatever you do, don't stare into the statue's eyes for too long."

"I know that already."

"I'm just saying…people have died that way." Her concerned eyes glanced at him.

Talis swallowed hard, and followed her inside the cave. Gods, he didn't want to die like this. Farther in, the darkness was suffocating. He knew he had to walk boldly to survive the initiate's test, but as soon as he stepped onto a slippery stone, the feeling of snakes slithered at his feet. His heart skipped and thundered in his chest. *These are all just illusions*, he told himself. He couldn't trust his senses. But it was hard to ignore the feeling of hundreds of spiders crawling along his shoulders, and cold, slimy hands grasping at his legs. He wanted to kick them away, but he had to keep going.

When he tried to breathe, he couldn't. It was like there was no air in the cave. *This is all an illusion…part of the Rites.* He controlled his desire to gasp like a fish caught out of water. After he pictured the morning sun rising over the desert, the vision calmed him, and he took deeper breaths.

Around a curved corner came the glimmer of an eerie green light. Talis stopped, his legs refusing to take another step. His blood thumped hard through his temples. Two ghostly-green, glowing orbs hovered in the darkness. In between stood a statue of the terrifying Zagros, in a battle-stance, wielding an executioner's blade in one hand, and in the other he held hundreds of tiny, severed heads tied together by a string. The onyx statue of the Lord of the Underworld. His mouth was open wide, tongue stretched out. Talis felt the hairs stand up along the back of his neck. The statue was revolting.

A cloaked figure in black knelt before the statue, mumbling prayers. Golden orbs floated in the air all around the chamber. Candles were lit around the kneeling figure, giving off a freakish, flickering light. Mara grabbed Talis's arm, and they hid behind a boulder and bent down, straining to listen.

"...I vow," the figure said, "that my father, his soul find shall find respite. The endless war of Nyx—spare him, oh great Zagros, please spare him for such a fate."

Mara leaned close to Talis. "It's Rikar," she whispered. Rikar? What was he doing here? He was a foul-tempered student of the Order of the Dawn and sparring partner with Nikulo.

After she spoke, Rikar whirled around and glared at them. His eyes glowed green for a moment and then dimmed to black. "You dare violate the sanctity of this temple?"

Mara and Talis stepped out from the shadows, bathed in the violent green light glowing around the statue. Rikar raised a hand and Talis felt a sickening energy creep up his legs and into his stomach, squeezing hard until massive bursts of pain shot through his body. What kind of strange magic was Rikar using on him?

"Stop it!" Mara hissed, glowering at Rikar. "Leave it for the Blood Dagger competition."

Talis gasped and coughed as the pain diminished. He balled up a fist and started to charge at Rikar but Mara held him back.

"I won't even need to use a drop of magic against you pathetic runts." Rikar stood and strode past them, shoving Talis aside. "Nice to see you're all better, Your Royal Highness. I look forward to using my sword to make you injured again." He chuckled, pulling his cloak over his head and stormed out.

"What was that all about?" Mara shook her head. "Why was he in here, anyway?"

"I really don't want to know... Rikar has acted incredibly strange since his father died."

Mara shuddered, as if a cold chill had fallen over her. "Didn't you used to be friends? What happened to him?" Talis wished he knew, but Rikar always failed to talk with him about what had happened.

Turning aside, she took a deep breath and faced the onyx statue, as if filled with a new resolve. "We have to complete the rites of initiation, and do it quickly." She beckoned him towards the shrine, and they knelt together on the outer ley line. After their knees touched the ley lines, a faint green light rose and strengthened into a blistering blaze that Talis could feel in his legs.

He studied the burning eyes and deep crevices on the god's face, and approached the statue, his gaze fixed on the dark lord. He had to remain fearless, or else he knew a demon might take possession of his mind. As he steadied himself, he thought of his brother, Xhan, dead many years ago. He was free now, free of the heavy burden of life. Xhan rested with loved ones, along the Fair Seas... Talis had to believe that. Wasn't his soul free?

Closer to the statue, Talis stretched out his trembling hand. The god's tongue was cold and wet as Talis touched it, and soon the feeling of a miasmic fire slithered down his arm. In an instant, a vision possessed his mind. He saw a dimly lit cave filled with black tangle vines. A green fire raging under an iron pot. Eyes hard and ruthless, staring at him in the chamber. Talis felt like his life was slowly being drained away by the demonic eyes. This was it, he knew he was dying.

Mara was wrong, worshipping Zagros didn't bring them favor. Worshiping the God of Darkness only brought a demon's attention upon them. He was a fool for making this vow with Mara.

4

The Order of the Dawn

The Temple dedicated to the pantheon of gods, constructed by the magical Order of the Dawn over a thousand years ago, gleamed in the morning sunlight as Talis sauntered up the cobblestone street. Today he would study with Master Viridian, the leading wizard of the Order, for a chance at breaking his many year long failing streak, his inability at casting magic. Not that Talis was optimistic today. Especially since every time he'd tried in the past the results had proved disastrous.

"Another day, another failure?" Rikar said, and tipped his black, bulbous hat as he swaggered inside the Order's gate. Talis scowled, feeling the fury well up inside over Rikar's use of dark magic on him at the Temple of Zagros. Twin wizards standing watch at the entrance made notes, studying the students as they paraded inside. They frowned in suspicion at Talis as he approached.

Talis ignored Rikar's taunting eyes, and gathered up his red robes and stepped over the stone dragons that guarded the gates. The sandy courtyard inside was raked in clean, diagonal lines that marked the ley lines of the world, divined by the geomancers of the Order. Talis skirted along the edges of the courtyard, following habits of caution, daring not to taint the central lines that marked the middle of the yard. But he was one of the few that followed the cautious course, as others, Rikar and Nikulo included, trampled where they liked, seemingly oblivious of what lay underneath. Arrogant fools.

"Ah…good morning, young master Talis." Mistress Cavares, an old, eccentric wizard, stopped in the courtyard and stared at him with curious and concerned eyes. Talis wasn't sure what she taught (or her area of mastery), but he knew the rest of the students and wizards tried their best to stay away from her. She came closer and ran fingers across her wrinkled lips.

"You look…in a dark mood today. Has something happened?"

Talis stiffened at her words, picturing the onyx statue of Zagros, and he felt a wind whip up and spike along his shoulders. "I have studies with Master

Viridian this morning," he mumbled, and glanced at Mistress Cavares.

"I see..." She frowned as if considering something. "Well, on your way. Do go see a healer if you're not feeling well."

Talis bowed and scurried away, not wanting to be late, but more than anything, he wanted to avoid talking to Mistress Cavares. Soon he reached the thick mahogany door leading to the masters' chambers, and he climbed stairs that wound up and around, splashes of sunlight warming portraits of the old, renowned masters from the Order's more glorious days.

He finally reached the top level of the building. Down the marble corridor he strode, the view of the City of Naru flickering in through windows, the glare blinding him temporarily until his eyes adjusted to the light.

"Come along in here," Master Viridian whispered from a side room.

Talis's eyes were blind to the dark now, and he could barely see his Master or the details of the room inside. He bumbled his way forward, and bumping into the doorframe gave him enough time for his eyes to adjust to the candle-filled chamber.

Master Viridian levitated two feet above the ground, his legs crossed, eyes closed in meditation. His black and silver beard was forked in two, each beard tip tied with a sun-medallion shaped of gold. The Master's pale grey eyes opened, and stared at Talis with a long, intense look. His eyes looked even more washed out than usual, and Talis thought it was because the Master spent too much time staring at the sun in an attempt at absorbing its power.

"Close the door, please. Yes, thank you. Now choose a place to meditate." Master Viridian gestured at the silk pillows scattered on a rug embroidered with an ornate illustration of the sun. Something about his master's voice made Talis move quickly, an urgency driving his movements. Was there something wrong?

Talis obeyed and found a gold pillow and sat crossing his legs. The light dimmed instantly so that Talis could barely see the room. After his eyes adjusted to the darkness, Talis swore he glimpsed ghostly faces staring at them from each of the four, misty corners of the room.

The walls had disappeared, and in their place, a grey fog expanded out into nothingness.

"Don't pay attention to the room…pay attention to what's inside your mind. Close your eyes, close your mind to the room. Find the brilliant speck of light that is the sun."

Soon sunlight roared in Talis's mind and he relished in the feeling of its warm glow on his face. He knew he was now inside the world of dreams, the world where he felt free, where he'd journeyed to thousands of times before. This was a familiar exercise for Talis: find the sun, find the wind, find the lightning and the thunder, find the rain and the cool mountain spring, feel the earth…your hands plunged into wet, loamy soil. The core pathways leading to elemental magic.

"Now raise your hands to the sun and let the rays burn your palms until they are black, charred, smoking, angry… Feel the fire pulsing and radiating from your palms until the flames lap out, hungry, thirsty, parched, needing wind and substance to devour."

Talis did as his Master commanded and his palms burned and pain shot down his arms, but he resisted the desire to recoil his hands and instead kept them steady. In a matter of seconds flame tendrils danced out from his palms like the many intertwining arms of Kaleria, The Laughing God, who makes light of all mortal ambition and power.

"Be careful, contain the flames lest they burn you up inside… Form a balance between the wind outside and the heat inside. Push enough of the flames outside to keep yourself from overheating... Avoid the path that leads to death."

Images of charred and burning wizards after past battles flashed in Talis's mind. He knew well the rules of magic and the high costs of ignoring its limits. That was the main reason he feared Fire Magic, and he guessed, was probably why he had failed to produce it.

But despite his fears, his concentration allowed him to control the flow and he continued to allow the flames to pour from his hands. It was easier here, inside the world of dreams, to cast magic.

"Excellent...I salute your progress. Now see me, see the grey fog, see the room, bring the flames here, to me. The fog is wind, use its latent power to fuel the flame's anger, and burn me up. Know well in your mind that the flames can never harm me."

Talis found his eyes flared open and the room seemed instantly smaller. He felt a surge of heat in his palms. Something sputtered from his hands and tiny puffs of smoke filled his nostrils. Fear coursed through his body and his concentration broke. The feeling of heat in his body stopped cold. He grimaced, knowing he'd failed yet again at producing Fire Magic.

"That was a reasonably good attempt, I suppose." Master Viridian's face twitched, and his eyes looked disappointed. "I still sense fear in you, fear of fire, fear of yourself, even. Tis a shame you can't release your fears into the void."

Master Viridian sighed and rubbed his nose with the back of his hand, then stared at his fingers like he'd found ink spilled on his knuckles. "Let me ask you a question. How did you manage to overcome your fear of fighting with swords? Don't you have a battle ahead at the Blood Dagger competition? From what I understand, although I've never seen fights such as those in the arena, the fighting is fierce... Blood is drawn and magical healers often fail to cure wounds. Am I correct?"

Talis nodded, realizing the connection to casting magic. He pictured the last time he'd battled in the arena and the battle stances he'd used, and he spoke the words of his twin modes of martial power, "Wear the Battle Mask and Slay the Demon..."

"Is this part of your training?"

"To overcome fear of injury and pain, wearing the battle mask is our mental protection, and slaying the demon keeps us focused on destroying our enemy...the demon in our minds."

"Where is your fear while you battle?" Master Viridian allowed a smile to raise the corners of his lips.

"Slain...fear is the demon. How we slay the demon is to execute the movements. Dancing Butterfly,

Cringing Monkey, Leaping Snake, Dragon Circles the Moon… We memorize many martial movements, train and train and train until they are habits, then in the arena the fight is against our fear and emotions…and besting our enemies."

Master Viridian chuckled, light filling his eyes. "Sounds like the way wizards learn battle magic. Do you see the connection? Good, I can feel it in your eyes. And who are you fighting at the Blood Dagger competition?"

"We're fighting Rikar and Nikulo…tomorrow." Was it so close already? Talis pictured the haughty gaze in Rikar's eyes this morning, and scowled, wishing he could wipe that expression off his face.

"If you apply the same principles you've learned in melee fighting to casting magic, you'll do just fine. Don't think producing magic is anything different, treat it much the same."

Except that losing control of magic could cause you to explode and kill everyone around you, Talis thought. He bowed to Master Viridian, keeping his fears to himself.

"Thank you, Master, I will try." If he could only get the image of burned wizards out of his head. Then perhaps he could succeed at casting magic.

Instead of staying after school to study, as his masters had admonished him to do, Talis snuck out of the Order through a side, secret tunnel. He made his way to the Royal Finishing School where Mara was supposed to be learning how to act like a proper young lady of the court. Not that she was a good student.

She drove her teachers crazy with questions like, *Why do ladies have to act so stupid?* And when her manners teacher dared to suggest that Mara give up hunting and fighting, Talis had to talk her out of pouring a trick farting potion in her tea. The effect of the potion usually lasted an entire week. Even though Talis chuckled at the idea, he knew it would just get Mara into even worse trouble.

The stone wall surrounding Mara's school was easy to scale, and Talis climbed down wisteria vines and crept over to hide behind a statue of the Goddess Nestria, the Ruler of the Sky. He tossed a pebble at the window of the large room where Mara and several other young girls were practicing the art of dancing. Mara glanced outside, squinting as she spotted Talis. Then she returned her attention back to her teacher, and nodded and curtsied in response.

After finishing several more elegant spins, leaps, and hand flourishes, the girls in the class bowed to the teacher and filed out of the room in a graceful dance.

Talis snuck around to the side door where Mara had escaped at his previous visits, and waited for her. If he was in luck today, dancing might be her last class.

Around ten minutes later the door squeaked open and Mara's devilish eyes peeked through.

"You just couldn't wait to see me, could you? You know my teachers will kill you if they find you in here again."

"Come on, let's get out of here." He grinned, noticing that she had already changed. "We've got to talk about the Blood Dagger competition… you know it's tomorrow. The Tame Shrew?" Talis lifted his fist to his mouth, as if drinking.

"I couldn't think of a nastier, seedier tavern to plot our battle strategy against Rikar and Nikulo… Absolutely perfect." Mara beamed with exuberant eyes and came closer. She stretched out her fingers and brushed a lock of Talis's hair away from his forehead. He felt a shiver run through him from where she touched his face. She glanced around to see if anyone was looking, and kissed him quickly on his cheek. She seized Talis's hand and they made their way through the bushes and up and over the wall.

The afternoon sun filtered through the olive leaves, casting quivering inky shadows across the cobblestone street. The lazy windless time of day when many citizens took naps or drank milk tea and played cards. Talis and Mara snuck along the winding corridors of upper Naru until they found the door that led down through the darkness to Shade's Gate and out into Fiskar's Market. Old men and women sat about sighing disdainfully and chatting with each other in nostalgic tones. They glanced suspiciously at Talis and Mara as they darted through the market.

Back behind the market stalls, down a dank and smelly side corridor, they found The Tame Shrew, one of the oldest and least respectable taverns in Naru. Outside the faded red tavern door stumbled two old drunks locked in a cheerful arm-grasp. They teetered about precariously singing well-sung songs of war and adventure. Talis and Mara skirted around the duo and made their way inside the dark tavern.

Conflicting smells overpowered them as they entered: sweat and ale and roses. The tavern owner's wife had a rooftop garden where she grew many fragrant varieties of roses, and she clipped the strongest-smelling ones and kept them in an old, ceramic vase on the middle of the bar. Despite her earnest attempt at eliminating the other foul smells in the tavern, the stench remained.

"There's a quiet table over in the corner." Mara stepped down the stairs and squeezed past a man and a woman having a furious argument. Talis thought it sounded like a lover's quarrel.

As Talis sat next to Mara, the woman fighting with the man burst into tears and stomped out of the tavern, leaving the man to stare stupidly at the mug of ale he was holding.

"I don't supposed he'll be standing after a few hours," Mara whispered, a grin playing on her mouth.

"Two hours at the most." Talis motioned a serving girl over to their table. "Could we have two honey meads?"

Mara's eyes lit up and she smacked her lips in anticipation. "And a slice of chocolate and raspberry cake?"

The serving girl eyed Mara disdainfully, but she twisted around and stomped back behind the bar and filled two mugs with golden brew from a barrel.

"She doesn't like me much..." Mara scrunched up her eyes and lips in imitation of the serving girl's pouty expression.

Talis chuckled, most girls despised Mara, something about her came off as wrong to them. She acted like she wanted to take every ideal for how a girl should live and smash those ideals with her own contempt. And that was exactly why he liked her so much.

"So you think we can beat Rikar and Nikulo?" Mara accepted a mug of mead from the serving girl, and frowned, peering at the kitchen.

"Don't get all upset… I'll have yer cake out soon enough." The serving girl muttered to herself and charged off again after giving Talis his mug.

"Honestly?" Talis took a swig of the sweet honey mead—gods it tasted like heaven. "I don't think we have a chance of winning against them. The question is, can we survive long enough to keep from getting murdered by Rikar? How many people has he killed in previous competitions?" Although Talis knew magical healers stood ready to cast healing spells on injured combatants, sometimes nothing could done, like the time Rikar sliced off a combatant's head.

"You're so optimistic…" Mara rolled her eyes in disgust. "Maybe I'll visit the old witch that sells curses after all. And here I am, drinking my mead and thinking we could actually win."

Talis poked her affectionately in the arm and grinned. "Here comes your cake…thank you, miss… Go on, eat up, don't make a face. You'll feel better with the chocolate swirling around in your belly."

"I'll feel better holding the Blood Dagger and displaying it to my father and mother." Mara gulped down a bite of cake and squeezed her eyes closed in delight. "Mmm, I can picture it so clearly... Mother, Father, I've won, and there is no way I'm marrying Baron Delar's fat old warthog of a son."

She suddenly opened her eyes and fixed her gaze on Talis. "You will do all you can to help me win, won't you? I really mean it. I've known you forever and then some, and if anyone can help me out of this—situation—you're the one."

Talis swallowed another gulp of mead, and nodded, unable to break away from the sight of Mara's earnest eyes. He would do anything to help her, and besides, winning against arrogant Rikar would be more of a prize than the Dagger itself.

If he survived.

5

The Blood Dagger

Talis sensed Mara stalking up behind him as he stared up at the stone arena on the day of the Blood Dagger competition. Stars twinkled through the black velvet sky filling him with hope and energy for their upcoming battle. The familiar scent of roses wafted over him, the scent of Mara and the scent of House Lei's famous flower gardens.

"I prayed to the gods, to Zagros, Nyx, Nacrea, and to Nestria." He turned and smiled at Mara as she approached with a look of trepidation on her face.

"What say the heavens?" She gazed up at the four moon sisters, reaching out like she could caress the stars. When she moved her fingers, starlight seemed to coalesce around her hands. In that moment, Talis realized how beautiful she was and a part of him ached to hold her and keep her safe.

The moons were splayed across the sky, speaking of a secret. The Diviners of the Celestials would call the moons' alignment "The Three Sisters Conspiring

Against the Brilliant One." The cruel plot against the one of light. Fate was strong today, for or against you. Talis frowned and felt like even the stars were trying to dissuade him from this battle.

He and Mara had been a sparring team for seven years, ever since he'd survived the initiation allowing him to wield the blade at six years old. This was a contest for reputation and favor, and the right to compete in the Arena of the Sej Elders. As Mara hoped for, it would mean she could get her wish and ask her parents to call off the marriage between her and Baron Delar's son. If they failed to grant Mara her wish the Lei family would risk disfavor from the gods. For Talis, he hoped that winning would mean praise and recognition from his father, praise he'd failed to receive.

Mara twirled her twin nine-inch blades, and paused, staring at them with satisfaction. She handled them like her precious pets. "Be careful of Rikar's twirling strike. Go for a foot sweep if you see him start to spin."

Talis thought of Rikar's deadly dances at previous matches, where he broke bones, sliced off arms and legs and hands, and even in one case, severed a head. That time the healer couldn't do a thing to save the boy's life, not even with magic. Talis wanted to be brave, but bloody images of contestants at previous matches flashed in his mind.

"Are you ready?" he aimed his short sword at the arena's standard flapping in the breeze. Mara brandished her daggers at the flag as well, a look of intense determination beaming from her eyes.

At least one of them felt confident. They strode into the arena, the House of the Warrior, and smelled air thick with cedar and sweet incense. Hairs stood up along Talis's arms and he clenched his jaw to keep his teeth from chattering. The dark, silver and grey stones shimmered as if recently washed, catching the torchlight along the tunnel leading into the circular arena.

Inside the combatant's circle, a round opening above allowed moonlight to shine onto the sandy floor. Great two-handed swords and halberds and spiked shields were mounted along the stone wall. Torches flickered in between the weapons, whipped by the wind. His cheeks stung from the cold and he wished he were warming his hands by a fire. A freshly painted red line had been drawn around the circle, marking the boundaries of the contest.

The arena was quiet and empty, except for Nikulo and Master Jarvis Numerian, a giant of a man, muscles rippling underneath his banded leather armor. A twisted scar marred his otherwise noble face. Talis felt relieved that Jarvis, who was friendly to House Storm, judged today's match. Perhaps they had a chance after all.

"We challenge the undefeated for the right to hold the Blood Dagger," Talis shouted, and glanced around, hating the fact that Rikar always entered the arena at the last moment, part of his strategy to intimidate opponents.

Nikulo strode forward, his protruding belly jiggling from side-to-side, and clapped his studded leather armor. He pointed the bladed tip of his metal staff at Talis and Mara, his face scowling and eager. Somehow Talis didn't feel so threatened. Although Nikulo was a strong competitor, Rikar was the malevolent one.

"Do we have a complete team to battle the challengers?" Jarvis spread his arms wide.

Footsteps pounded down the tunnel, and Rikar came charging into the arena, his face shiny and proud, hair slick and wet as if he'd just taken a bath. His eyes mocked Talis. *I'd like to ram a sword's tip deep into your eye socket,* Talis thought.

"Do I have to fight these two buffoons?" Rikar snorted.

Talis gripped his sword so hard his fingers burned. *We used to be friends,* Talis thought. But after Rikar's

66

father had died, signs of friendship ended. All because Talis's father had refused to grant the Rite of Royal Blood to Rikar's dead father. This lack of performing the royal rites meant the Lords of the Underworld had condemned Rikar's soul to the torture of the Grim March. And now Rikar hated Talis. It was unfair and unjustified. Talis hadn't done anything to Rikar, but his old friend made him feel like he was the one responsible.

Mara stepped towards Rikar and brought a dagger across her throat, a look of malice on her face.

Rikar chuckled. "This little one can't wait to get her hands on me. I can't say I blame her."

"I challenge you for the right to wield the Blood Dagger," Talis shouted. "And the Blood Dagger we shall hold"—he flushed, trying to remember the words—"we shall hold until the spring bud kisses the maple tree." He raised his sword and aimed at the zenith.

Jarvis harumphed. "Then begin… And fight until one of you is wounded—severe enough to require intervention by the healer. From that, I will announce the winner." He gestured at shadows so dark that Talis couldn't see a thing. "Master Healer Nonce, if you please, we are ready to begin."

A bald man in a blood-red robe emerged from the blackness and shuffled towards them. He peeled an orange, not even bothering to look up. Although healers cured many wounds with magic, sometimes nothing could be done. It was known as *"The fate of the sword."* Talis pictured the boy who'd had his head hacked off, and touched his neck, feeling the blood pulsing through his veins. He swallowed hard and glanced at the shimmering edge of Rikar's blade. In Naru, law allowed the sword to choose the strong over the weak.

From the crazed look in Rikar's eyes, Talis knew he meant to inflict as much pain as possible. And Nikulo twirled his bladed staff so fast it hummed. Rikar whirled his curved sword around in a flourish, raised a finger and summoned a huge, shimmering blade above his head. Talis felt his skin go clammy, wishing he could cast magic like that. Memories of his failed attempt at magic yesterday with Master Viridian flashed in his mind's eye.

"No magic in the arena." Jarvis scowled at Rikar. "You know the rules."

Rikar strode towards Talis, spinning his sword deftly. "Ready to scream, boy?"

Talis gritted his teeth and ignored his taunts. He circled around to his left, and Mara followed his lead, staying close.

Rikar's blade sung as it cut through the air, just inches from Talis's stomach. Talis clasped a hand over hit gut, almost feeling the blade lash into his body. *A few inches closer and my intestines would be spilling out onto the sand,* Talis thought.

While Rikar leered at Talis, distracted by several quick strikes from Talis's sword, Mara leapt at Rikar's back and punctured his scale mail armor just above the hip on the side. Blood dripped from her dagger, and for a moment, her face flashed a triumphant look.

Rikar whirled around and kicked Mara on the shoulder, sending her tumbling through the air. She fell hard on her back and whimpered. A cold sweat fell over Talis as he remembered her being injured by the boar. He charged Rikar, hoping to catch him unaware, but Rikar just parried and deflected his sword aside.

Talis sighed in relief as Mara pushed herself up and grabbed her daggers, nodding as if she were okay.

Rikar clapped his sword against the bloodied spot on his armor. "You barely pricked me. Next time shove your dagger in a bit harder…." He scoffed, and motioned for Nikulo to charge Talis.

Nikulo grunt as he darted forward, spinning wide slices with his staff, causing Talis to leap back. Talis thrust his sword at Nikulo's chest, but Nikulo swatted the weapon aside, spun, and slammed the side of his staff against Talis's shins, knocking Talis face-first onto the ground.

Stars spun wildly in his eyes. To the right, Talis could see Rikar raising his blade. In a smooth strike Rikar brought the sword down on him, but Talis rolled aside just in time. Mara, catching Rikar completely unprepared, jumped on his back and tightened a dagger against his throat. A line of blood trickled down his neck as he sank to his knees, face red and sweaty.

Rikar growled. With one lightning-quick move, he pulled down her dagger arm and sent her tumbling over his shoulder and onto the ground.

A whirl of wind caused Talis to move and jump to his feet, just in time to avoid Nikulo's bladed staff. He quick-stepped, parried and spun around, then slashed at Nikulo's ribs but he knocked the blade away. Nikulo grinned in satisfaction raising his blade-tip towards him. Talis tensed and leapt at Nikulo, swinging his blade at Nikulo's head. Nikulo raised his staff to block, but Talis kicked his chest and knocked him onto his back.

With Nikulo out of the way, Mara and Talis charged Rikar in unison. Talis sprang at Rikar, while Mara circled around. *We can win,* Talis thought. He thrust his blade at Rikar's chest, but somehow Nikulo had managed to get up quickly, and drove right through Talis and Mara, his bladed staff spinning wide. Talis jumped away, only to feel Rikar's sword grating along the surface of his ring mail chest armor, issuing a shower of sparks. Talis retreated fast, the smell of metallic smoke lingering in the air.

Grinning, Rikar pressed his advantage, slicing and pushing him back towards the arena's edge. As Rikar was about to land a blow on Talis's neck, a dizzy sensation washed over Talis's mind. All movement around him stopped, and the light in the arena went gold. The sky glittered with dancing stars.

As if the world had frozen, Talis could see the entire scene at once. The weakness in Rikar's defense. Rikar's frozen face shone with hate and bloodlust and madness. And soon Talis felt a wind whirling inside his chest.

He knew instantly where he had to strike.

Time rushed on and Talis danced aside and landed a blow hard on Rikar's hip, breaking through his armor, sending blood spurting, a red stain bubbling along his leg. Rikar sank, gripping the wound. That was it. The pain shot up to Rikar's eyes and across his face. He bit his lip hard and sank to the ground. Talis grinned. Rikar was finished.

The healer cried out and raced forward. He placed his hands on Rikar's hip and the armor glowed white-hot, and Rikar's face was filled with light. Rikar's reddened eyes glared furiously at Talis.

"The winner of this year's Blood Dagger is Talis of House Storm and Mara of House Lei." Master Jarvis nodded to them both and raised their hands in victory.

Talis found that a smile had spread across his face. They'd won. They really done it this time and gained the prize. Father would finally see him as worthy to carry on the Storm family lineage. And Mara would get her wish. Relief and pride poured over him as he gazed into Mara's eyes and clasped his arms around her in a long, triumphant hug.

She whispered in his ear, "I knew we could do it. You were amazing, Talis. The best I've ever seen you fight. Thank you so much for fighting for me. It means the world to me."

He nodded, a torrent of emotions flooding through him at her words. They'd won the Blood Dagger and won the right to fight in the Arena of the Sej Elders. In front of all the crowds that gathered to watch the fights. Talis remembered his father's beaming face after his older brother Xhan had won his first Blood Dagger competition. It was his turn to earn Father's pride. He couldn't wait to run home and tell his family.

The healer finished casting the binding spell and sealed Rikar's wounds. Talis walked over and offered a hand to help him to his feet, but Rikar slapped his arm away. "Don't you dare touch me." He picked up his weapon and limped off and disappeared down the tunnel.

Talis looked over at Mara, and gripped her hand. "I didn't think we had a chance. But you were so amazing."

Mara blushed, and waved the idea away. "You finished him. What got into you anyway?"

"It was nothing. I got in a lucky strike." Talis could feel a redness wash over his face.

"You've improved." Nikulo stared at Talis, as if puzzled. "That was an incredible move at the end."

Master Jarvis Numerian tromped over to where they had gathered. "That was a good fight. They outplayed you both at first"—he studied Nikulo and Talis—"but your final blow...deadly fast and accurate."

Talis bowed to Master Jarvis, still feeling lightheaded over the win. As Jarvis marched away, Talis turned to leave with Mara, noticing the air was somehow warmer now. Mara reached out and held Talis's hand and they strode out of the arena and made their way down the narrow cobblestone street, where tall shops pressed in from either side.

"You kept your promise to protect me, Talis." Mara glanced up at him, pride and gratitude in her eyes.

Talis squeezed her hand and grinned at her, his head bobbing from side-to-side. "I meant it when I said I'd do anything for you." He started to speak but she pressed a finger over his mouth, an undecipherable look on her face. Her hands slid down to the sides of his face and she leaned her head against his chest as if wanting to hear his heart beating. She stayed like that for a while, while Talis found himself nervous and uncertain of what to do next.

He had to say something. "Want to eat a little before we go home? I'm starving."

She separated and gave him an assuring, disappointed smile, then turned and sauntered with him hand-in-hand all the way to their favorite bakery. The air smelled of sweet pies from the baker's oven, with wafts of apple and honey and pear stirring in his nostrils. His stomach complained. As they went to go inside the bakery, a small, dirty boy in shoddy clothes ran up to Talis.

"Please sir, have pity on an old lady and her grandson." The boy gestured to a frail, wrinkled woman crumpled against a stone house. Her hair looked windswept and tangled, and her skin was sunburnt and dry.

Talis wanted to go inside and celebrate with her, but the boy wouldn't let him pass.

"Wait," Mara said, and held Talis's shoulder. She turned to face the boy. "Where are you from?"

"We're refugees...from the city of Onair. Please, sir, just a few coppers?"

"Onair?" Talis said. His father was from the city of Onair, far to the west along the sea. Why were there refugees coming here in from Onair? Last time he had talked with his father, he heard that the city thrived with trade and from the production of rugs and dyes and silk.

"She looks hungry," Mara said, then lowered her voice to Talis. "And very sick, like she's dying."

The boy's voice was desperate. "I wouldn't ask for myself. But my grandmother is so cold. I'm afraid for her life."

"We should help her… Give her some coins."

Talis nodded, and glanced at the cringing woman as they approached. Mara put out her hand. "Please, we mean no harm." The woman blinked, breathing in and out haltingly as she switched her stare from Talis to Mara.

"You see," Mara said, "my friend here has a few extra coins… We wanted to share them with you. It's cold outside."

Opening her mouth as if to speak, the old woman coughed several times instead, wincing as if something hurt on the inside. She took in a long, halting breath, and lifted her moist eyes to gaze at Mara. "It *is* cold outside. Cold, cold, so cold…" A tear spilled down her cheek, but she remained motionless.

Talis placed some coins into her shriveled hands. They were like ice, as if nothing could ever warm that flesh. The woman stared at the coins for a while, then smiled at Talis. "You're a kind boy. I've not had such kindness since"—she glanced off—"since before..." Her voice trailed off, and her eyes glazed over.

Turning to the boy, Talis said, "What's happened in Onair?"

"We came with the others that escaped. All is lost now, lost to the waves."

"To the waves?" Mara said.

"Aye, to the fury of the sea. When our rulers refused to yield to the Jiserians, their sorcerers sent a tide such has never been seen to destroy our walls."

Jiserians? Naru was allied with the Jiserian Empire. He thought of his father telling stories of his childhood in Onair, along the beautiful sea. What would Father do if he knew that Onair had fallen to the Jiserians? Surely Naru would break their alliance and fight to help defend those in Onair.

"And the necromancers came and sent hordes of undead into our city, killing the innocent and the foolish. We were all fools for not leaving earlier."

A cold shudder swept through Talis as he imagined an undead army ravaging the seaside city. He'd seen drawings of them inside books of legend and myth. Ghosts roaming the frozen forests to the north, animating slain humans and animals, their lifeless bodies filled with demonic spirits. Those stories still terrified and excited him at the same time. The dark arts of necromancery were banned in Naru.

"You must come and stay with my family, until you're well—"

The boy interrupted Talis with his raised palm. "We cannot. I thank you, I do. But we cannot bring curses upon your house."

The old woman gazed at a shadow scarring the stone street. Her head trembled like she was possessed by a fit of terror. A drip of spittle fell from her gaping mouth. Talis felt a great fear seize up in his chest and from Mara's fearful eyes he knew she felt the same way.

Despite the words of assurance that Talis said to her, the old woman just stared at the ground, ignoring the world around her. The shadow of darkness *did* seem to cast over her, and nothing could lift it.

"I want to go," Mara whispered. "Take me away from here. I want to go home."

As they left, Talis stopped a moment, studying the spot where the old woman stared. In the dark form, where the shadow merged with the light, he swore he noticed a shape: a wraith. Its ghastly eyes seemed to pierce his soul.

6

The Ancient Struggle

In the fires of the great kitchen of his house, Talis pictured the image of the wraith he'd just seen. Although the room was warm, he felt a chill so strong his arms trembled. He gazed at the flames, remembering the story of the siege of Onair. His mind drifted off, and all he could see were the hideous scenes from his nightmares. The ones where fingers gripped his neck so hard he'd wake up coughing. Darkness and fire intermingled. The sound of wicked laughter ringing in his ears.

"Are you all right?" His mother, Nadean, placed her palm over his forehead as if to see whether he had a fever.

Talis snapped his attention back and smiled at her. What was he worried about? They'd just won the Blood Dagger competition. He couldn't wait to tell them the news, but he had to do it at the right time.

"I'm fine, I'm just thinking about something, that's all."

Mother went back to preparing dinner, though her concerned eyes glanced at him a few times. The spread on the table looked amazing: roasted pheasant, walnut and pear cake, spinach and garlic, and chicken bone soup. The delicious smells and the warmth of her smile made him relax, and he slowly felt the heat sink into his body.

Talis tensed as his father stomped into the room, his silver and black Elder's robes swishing, and his dark eyes gazing at the floor. *It's like we don't even exist,* Talis thought as he watched his father.

Garen Storm sat at the table with a thud, the chair croaking in response. He stared at the roast and frowned, as if expecting another dish.

"Problems with the negotiations?" Mother set an empty plate in front of him, and took his black hat to hang atop the coatrack.

Father brusquely rubbed his weathered face and pinched his eyes together. "Always troubles to deal with…" He sighed, glancing around the table. "A lost caravan, marauders in the desert, prices too high… And of course, if all that weren't enough, Viceroy Lei has decided to play politics again with the Order of the Dawn."

He studied Talis. "Someday these will be your concerns, son. To hold high the House of Storm."

Father made it sound like he was an ox carrying a burden. Talis nodded, pretending he was interested.

As if responding to Talis's expression, Father's eyes lit up and he leaned in towards Talis. "What we need is a small band of warriors to send those marauders to the Underworld"—he sliced the air with a finger—"a quick trip to Hell." He slapped his hand on the table and laughed like it was the best idea ever.

"I'd like to fight them." *Now was the perfect time to tell his father,* Talis thought.

"You?" Father raised an eyebrow. "Been practicing your sword techniques?"

"You could say that." Talis grinned. "Mara and I won the Blood Dagger competition today."

"What!" Father's face shone. "You two really won?" His brow furrowed. "Who did you fight?"

Talis groaned to himself. Father hadn't even bothered to find out who he was fighting, like he believed Talis didn't have a chance of winning. "We fought Rikar and Nikulo."

"Rikar? Madam Cheska's son? The cruel one?"

Talis nodded.

"Didn't he hack off an opponent's head in the training arena? He killed the poor chap... What a strange family." Father shook his head. "And you say you and Mara beat him?" He scoffed. "Well I suppose the gods of luck favored you today."

Talis flushed and clenched his fist. How could Father just dismiss his victory so easily?

"You won all the same. I suppose this calls for a celebration." Father glanced at his mother. "Let's plan something. Invite Mara and House Lei, if they'll come." He chuckled. "And perhaps a few friends."

"A party would be nice. It's been too long since…" Mother's voice trailed off and her face held a sad smile.

They remained quiet awhile, staring at the flames, until a flurry of pops from the fire startled them to attention.

"I suppose I'll retire to the study." Father stood and smiled pleasantly. "You did well, son. And you surprised me, you did. Not once did I suspect you'd win, but you did it." He turned, and strode off, nodding to himself. Talis, in that one moment, felt all the struggle was worth it. His father had finally praised him.

Later that night, around the hour that the dead call out to the living, Talis found himself unable to sleep, still feeling a buzzing in his stomach from winning the

Blood Dagger competition. His father's words of praise echoed in his mind. *You did well, son.*

He had to move. He felt an urge to go out and feel the night. So Talis snuck out and stalked through the dark streets of Naru, relishing the crisp cold air and the solace of the quiet past midnight. A meteor shot across the sky and Talis watched its blazing, shimmering trail fade into nothingness. Was it a message from Nestria, the Goddess of the Sky? He squinted, barely able to make out the observatory and the interconnected rings and spheres of the Temple of Nestria high atop the city. Why not go explore the city's highest point?

He spidered his way up the hill through back alleys and side streets, trying to avoid city guards and prying eyes. At the bare temple grounds situated at the top of Naru, the stars flooded down through the blackness. Below, the city shone pale-grey in the light of the four moons hanging in the sky. Talis glanced around, trying to spot any temple priests observing the stars. But only silence possessed the bleak landscape.

Now was the perfect time to practice his spell casting. He stared at the leaves racing across the ground, whipped up by the wind gusting in from the Nalgoran Desert far below.

He lifted his hands and let the coolness of the night air sharpen his mind. Remembering his training dreams, he focused on the leaves. *Remember the wind, remember the feeling of power swirling through you*, he thought. He stretched his long fingers towards the leaves, and exhaled a hissing breath through his teeth. Something flared up but then sputtered out weakly from his hands. There was wind from his hands, but not the kind that laid armies low. He pounded his fist on his forehead. Why couldn't he do magic?

He tensed his face and shouted at the leaves, as if the leaves could be moved by the sound of his voice. Would he ever learn? Would he ever gain the power of magic he so greatly craved?

"I doubt that will work," a low voice said from the shadows. Talis jumped, turning as Nikulo emerged from the darkness.

Talis flopped his arms at his sides. Bad enough that he'd failed, but worse still that Nikulo had been skulking out here, watching his ridiculous attempts.

"What are you doing out here?" Talis frowned at Nikulo and crossed his arms in defense.

"Relax...we're not in the Arena." Nikulo glanced up at the Observatory. "I couldn't sleep. My father was furious that we lost the Blood Dagger. All he does is push me to win."

Talis sighed, feeling the tension go out of his body. "I couldn't sleep either."

"How is that coming along?" Nikulo flourished his hands. *Why was he trying to help him?* Talis thought.

"How does it look." Talis sighed. "Nothing ever seems to work. I just don't get it."

"Keep at it." Nikulo studied Talis, his eyes black pools of curiosity. "Nothing worthwhile ever comes easy. You and Mara won today…that surprised me, and surprised Rikar as well. Soon enough you'll be casting spells. Just you wait and see."

"You think so?" Talis wasn't as sure. Three years he'd been in the Order of the Dawn and he still couldn't do magic outside of training dreams.

"I'll let you in on a secret. It took me four years before I cast my first spell. And that happened under the strangest circumstances."

Four years? Nikulo motioned him over towards the cliff's edge, and they walked together, until they could stare down out over the vast expanse of the Nalgoran Desert.

"I was assigned as a healer on a caravan, and we were attacked by desert marauders. I tended to a soldier's wound, but I couldn't staunch the flow of blood. No other healers were around and the man was dying in front of me. I panicked. Then something just flicked on inside and the next thing I knew my hands were glowing all red and I had this crazy feeling running through me. That was it. I'd used magic to save him."

"That sounds so easy."

"It's not like that. I'd been doing training dreams for years with my Master. So when the time came, I think all that training just kicked in."

Talis exhaled, more confused than ever. "I hope I'll figure it out soon."

Nikulo crinkled up his forehead and pointed at the sky. "That's weird." A slow-moving meteor was flying low. It left an enormous trail of smoke. But the meteor kept getting bigger and brighter.

It was coming towards them.

"What's that?" Talis bent low as the meteor sped faster until it roared over their heads and sped towards the city. Great bursts and crackles of orange and yellow and blue flame scintillated around the core. With a dull thud it exploded against the vast dome of the Temple of the Dawn. Embers burst into the air like millions of fireflies. He gaped, heart pounding, unable to move. After a few seconds, he felt a shock wave strike his chest and a rush of heat knocked him backwards.

7

Jiserian Invasion

Talis groaned and pushed himself up, gaping as the explosion crackled and roared across temple dome surface. His stomach clenched from the shock wave. Several smaller flaming meteors tore across the sky towards the temple. Those were no ordinary meteors... Talis knew what it was, it had to be Fire Magic.

Someone down in the city screamed amidst a flurry of shrieks and shouts and window shutters slamming open. Footfalls clapped on the cobblestone streets and figures raced through the dark while a plume of fire jetted across the sky. A deep, booming gong thundered out from the towers that kissed the highest point of Naru. The warning...the warning gong that sounded of an attack. Who was attacking them?

Talis and Nikulo stood gawking at the rippling explosions breaking out across the city. Overhead a flash of lightning singed the sky, shattering a guard tower. An enormous thunder cracked so loud that

Talis had to cover his ears. As students of the Order, they were sworn to protect the temple at all costs. Talis and Nikulo jolted to action, and dashed down towards the temple.

They reached the street and followed it snaking down and around the hill past soldiers burdened with steel armor, past citizens crying in terror at skies aflame, past howling dogs and cowering cats. Nearing the temple, Talis spotted wizards from the Order of the Dawn flying high above. Sprouts of fire erupted from their palms, spiraling across the sky, engulfing a menacing cloud of writhing shadows.

There, high in the sky, were dark sorcerers like the ones from Master Holoron's stories of legend and lore.

As Talis craned his neck up, searching the skies, he wondered how he could help. He heard a voice behind him.

"Over here," said Rikar. His hair sprung out in all directions under his nightcap. Mara stood next to him, staring with terrified eyes at the sky.

"What are you doing here?" Talis said, frowning at Mara.

"The explosion woke me up...I knew you'd be here—"

Talis interrupted. "But your parents will kill you if they know you're here."

"I don't care what my parents think! Our city is under attack. Let's do something to help."

At her determined voice, Talis shrugged and motioned towards the entrance. "Let's go up and get a better view." They climbed broad, marble stairs leading to the top of the temple. Torches lined the stone walls, sending shadows twisting eerily. As they neared the exit, brilliant flashes of orange and blue and golden light flooded through the shafts.

Outside, a shriek stopped Talis in his tracks. A wizard from the Order stood paralyzed, a shadow mist enveloping her form. *What in the name of the gods is afflicting her?* Talis wondered. Faces of demons rose and fell inside the mist, and when she sank to her knees, he spotted a dark sorcerer hovering in the sky fifty feet away from them.

"Over here." Rikar tensed his fingers and a luminescent blade, as long as a man, appeared in the air near the flying sorcerer. As Rikar swung his arm around the blade lopped the man in half. The cloud of shadows evaporated, releasing the woman from the spell, and the two halves of the sorcerer splatted on the streets far below.

"Help her," Talis shouted, and bent down next to the woman and held her wrist. She still had a weak pulse. They could save her.

Nikulo pushed Talis aside and lifted her up so she sat. Placing his hands on her upper back, golden light filled her body in waves. Her eyes surged open and she gasped as if waking from a nightmare.

"She'll be all right," Rikar said. "But we have to keep going."

They stayed low and jogged towards a group of young apprentices all clumped together, facing the sky. Fireballs and lightning and wind shot from their palms, finding purchase on sorcerers whirring about in the skies above.

"Cassis!" Rikar raced towards the group. Cassis, his close friend, turned and flashed him a terrified smile.

A thundering crack singed the air between them, pulverizing a twenty-foot stretch of wall. Talis smelled electricity and sulfur burning in the air. When the dust cleared, he noticed the wizards huddling together, their eyes fearful and desperate.

Rikar stretched out his fingers towards a sorcerer flying low over the group. A shimmering hammer formed in the sky, and he swung it around to strike him. The sorcerer jerked his eyes at Rikar as the weapon reflected off some invisible shield, and with a flick of his wrist knocked Rikar back ten feet, slamming his shoulders against the stone wall.

Nikulo darted towards Rikar and bent down, lifting his chin he felt for a pulse. Rikar shook his head, staring bleary-eyed around. He was still alive, thank the gods.

"Behind you!" Mara seized Talis and shook his shoulder.

Whirling around, Talis noticed an invader diving at him, malice burning in his red eyes. Cassis reacted, sending blast after blast of fireballs at the sorcerer. The sorcerer turned away from Talis, aiming his palms at her, and pressed the fire from her casting back to engulf her small form. Stretching her arms out, her body blazed as she breathed in and inhaled the power of the flames back inside. Soon she smoldered and her body was faintly lit now with an orange glow.

"You have to be careful, Cassis," shouted a boy next to her.

Her glance at him stopped her casting, and the enemy used the pause against her. He fired off waves of shadow and electricity, and the blast caught her in the stomach and wrenched her back, sending her electrified, twitching body tumbling across the ground. She swung her arms around, repelling the attack at last, and ignited the air in front of her in a shield of fire. Locked in battle, Cassis and the sorcerer pushed against each other until her face and chest and stomach glowed red. Steam swirled around her long, black hair and her body pulsed with some tremendous internal fire.

"Cassis stop…you have to stop it now!" yelled the apprentices. One grabbed her blazing arm but recoiled in pain. She was burning up inside.

When Talis saw the fire raging inside her, he could feel it circulating inside of his own body. Sweat flushed from his pores. He was as hot as an oven. Raging inside. He gazed at her, palms feverish. He wanted to help, he had to help her, and so he kissed the amulet dangling from his neck and made a prayer to the Goddess Nacrea, The Goddess of the Sun.

The sky was suddenly sallow and grey. Cassis's eyes were rigid in terror. The cowering apprentices frozen like statues. The sorcerer's face was fixed in a frightful glower. The explosions and shouts and cries ceased. A crack formed in the sky and a golden light blossomed from within the blackness. Now the fever inside Talis rose to a maddening intensity. It was far too much to bear. He stared at the sorcerer, knowing he had to release it.

With a hissing breath, he shot a powerful blast of fire from his palms. Since the invader had focused on Cassis, the burning blast incinerated the man and sent a shower of ash spreading across the sky. Smaller streams of fire from Talis had also released from his hands, a few nearing Cassis and the apprentices. Talis gaped. Was that magic? Had he done magic for the first time?

"What did you do?" Rikar yelled, fury spilling from his eyes.

Cassis screamed, panting, and flapped her fingers wildly, like she was trying to cool down. Her face glowed red like molten embers.

"Water...water," she gasped, and glanced around. The scintillating luminescence of fire raged inside her body.

Talis shielded his eyes from the intensity of light pouring from her body. Another sorcerer flew to them, as if drawn by the attack, and scowled at Talis. Cassis lifted her hands at the sorcerer, as if in a grave struggle against the hand of death itself. The sorcerer curled his fingers, aiming at him, and prepared to strike.

"No, Cassis, stop!"

Rikar ran in a hobble towards her, and in a brief glance at his face, Talis could see love and fury and a terrific sadness.

Despite the shouts of warning, Cassis released an enormous fireball at the enemy, vaporizing him in an instant. But she couldn't contain the power. It burned too strong inside. The light rose to a frenzied brilliance as many apprentices around her started running away.

Her neck dropped. Her flaming, brilliant body exploded in a powerful wave, burning chunks of fire and flesh searing everywhere around her.

Those fleeing nearby were cut down by the blast. Some were knocked against the stone walls. Some were blasted over the edge and plummeted helplessly to the ground far below. The ones refusing to leave her side were incinerated where they stood. Talis felt his stomach twist and flip around, and he vomited, coughing, choking on his own bile.

Gasping for air, for life, he tried to expel the image from his mind. A primal fear burrowed its way inside. What had just happened? Was this the terror of magic? He still felt the fire burning inside his body. Why would he risk his life and the lives of his friends? The power roared so strong. Could he ever learn to contain it? Or would he find a fate like that of Cassis?

Rikar balled up his fists and pounded the ground, sobbing. Nikulo came over and tried to comfort him, but Rikar just pulled away and curled up. A lightning bolt shattered a nearby tower, jolting them to attention. Rikar raised his head and stared blankly in the direction of the blast.

"She's gone," he whispered. "Why did Cassis have to die? Why does everyone I love have to die…"

"We'll be dead too if we don't get out of here." Mara pulled Talis back towards the stairs. "We have to go."

"Why of all times did you choose now to practice magic?" Rikar glowered at Talis, crawling towards him with murder in his eyes.

"It just happened—"

"It just happened? You cast a wild spell and obliterate the sorcerer and also hit your allies? Your inept, ill-targeted spell caused Cassis to lose her concentration, killing her and her friends? How does that *just happen*?"

"I didn't mean to hurt her…I was trying to help."

Mara turned Talis away from Rikar and urged him to leave. "Just ignore him, it wasn't your fault. Cassis went too far and lost control. Let's get out of here." She pointed at hundreds of black shapes charging across the sky. "Every moment more come—we're outnumbered. Let's go."

"Cowards," Rikar shouted, "I'd rather fight and die then run away like a dog. Don't you want to revenge her death?" Rage filled his eyes as he motioned to Nikulo, and they ran off towards the tower where a group of wizards were fighting a larger group of invaders.

"Listen to me, Talis. It wasn't your fault. And that spell you cast was amazing! I can't believe you cast Fire Magic. You completely murdered that sorcerer. And I mean it now, we have to get out of here. We simply can't compete against the kind of power they have." Mara sighed. "Let's at least try to find Master Viridian or one of the other masters."

But as they turned to leave, a sorcerer with flame-red hair flew towards them, his long black robe fluttering behind him. He blazing eyes burned black and gold as tracked their movements.

"Let's go!" Talis chased after Mara and they raced towards the stairwell, but he still felt those eyes boring into the back of his neck.

"Little mice, why are you running away?" the sorcerer said, his voice thick with malicious humor.

"The Master has sent me to collect you." He pointed a ruby-tipped staff at Talis and issued a flood of black tangle-vines.

8

The Surineda Map

Talis leapt out of the way, barely avoiding the choking vines, and tumbled down the dusty stairs. He regained his footing, and joined Mara in their descent, winding around and around until they reached the bottom. He could hear the sorcerer's laughter chasing after them.

"Oh good, a game of hide and seek... I always love a good game," the sorcerer said, his shrill and booming voice echoing down the stairwell.

Instead of going through the door leading out to the streets, Mara jumped back, shrieking, as a female sorcerer came in from the bottom entrance. Talis shoved the woman's back and she went sprawling onto a vase filled with peacock feathers.

"Down here!" Mara shot down into a dimly lit corridor that Talis knew led to the temple crypts. Why weren't the sorcerers attacking them? And who was this master that was trying to capture them?

Up ahead Talis could see eerie shadows dancing from the magical blue lights mounted along the walls.

The ancient crypts. The place of burial for thousands of departed wizards of the Order of the Dawn. Mara stopped at the bottom, and a luminescent face, the Door-Guardian, hovered in the air in front of a black iron and wooden door.

"Who goes there?" cried the guardian.

"Mara Lei, of House Lei." Mara pointed at Talis. "And Talis Storm, of House Storm. We seek refuge and safety inside the crypts."

"Refuge?"

"As in now!" Mara shouted. "We're being chased."

The guardian looked perplexed, as if trying to solve a puzzle. "How strange... Trouble here inside the temple?"

Footsteps rapped on the stone steps behind them, and voices chuckled fitfully. "Where have the little mice scurried off and hidden themselves? A game of hide-and-seek in the dungeon? Come back, little ones, our Master only wants to talk to you."

"I said *let us in*," hissed Mara. "Our lives are in danger."

As Mara pushed at the door, the portal bowed and blew golden dust at the door, illuminating the black iron on the surface. The dust revealed a complicated geometric pattern of overlapping triangles and circles.

The shapes moved and finally came together, and the door went *click* and opened.

They rushed inside and pounded down a stone ramp that led into a vast gloomy room, faintly lit by floating candles that spilled out a soft, orange light. Shadows flickered across grotesque faces, hundreds of stone figures, standing as guardians over the countless crypts of the fallen masters of the Order. Throughout the crypts, Talis could see countless silvery spider webs filling the air. The smell of mold and dust and embalming fluid pressed heavily like a choking hand.

Instead of the door slamming shut behind them, the voices following them got louder. "Of course we're allowed to enter," a sorcerer yelled. "No, no, we're not chasing them. Yes, we're friends. Be a good guardian and let us pass, now will you?"

Talis and Mara ducked behind a crypt statue and stared back at the door. They were going to take them away from Naru, Talis had heard stories like this. Dark sorcerers stealing children and raising them to study their nefarious black arts.

"Only royals and members of the Order may enter," the guardian said. "You're uninvited guests."

The door attempted to swing shut, but one of the sorcerers summoned a meaty hand the size of a man, and blocked the door from closing. The fat fingers flexed, snapping the door hinges.

"No," the guardian shouted, "you're not allowed to do that!"

"As if you can do anything about it," mumbled the red-haired sorcerer. He stepped inside the crypt. "Such flimsy magic here in Naru. One wonders why the Master allowed this pathetic city to remain neutral."

The other sorcerer, a tall, spindly woman in a silver robe, cast a spell, illuminating the crypts in a garish white light. "Do remain diligent, Calasar, these children must have some power if the Master has sent us after them."

"Mice? Oh, little mice?" Calasar shouted, "A bit of cheese, a bit of bread, a bit of red from your bloody head...."

"Don't scare them," the woman whispered. Then loudly, "We're not here to hurt you."

"Are we really only collectors then? Collectors for the Master? While the others are marauding the city, setting fire, sizzling innocent pets with lightning bolts, we're stuck down in all this gloom looking for a stupid boy?"

A boy? Talis thought. Why were they looking for him? He pointed at a mausoleum far off in the corner, and Mara nodded and followed him as he stalked away from the sorcerers. The white light from the sorceress disappeared and Talis stopped, waiting for his eyes to adjust to the darkness. Instead of voices, he heard only the lonely hiss of steam from an air vent. He continued creeping along, glancing at carvings of bulls and eagles and lions decorating the stone walls of the massive mausoleum.

At the base, he looked up and read the inscription: *Master Baribariso, Legendary Wielder of the Kalashi Sword, Undefeated in Battle, Yet Defeated by Old Age…*

"I've heard of him," Mara whispered, and traced her fingers over a carving of a lion with long fangs.

"Champion from an age long past. Do we dare hide inside?"

"This is a place of refuge."

"Mice chattering away… So easy to find you." Calasar lifted his fingers and aimed at Talis. "Don't make me hurt you."

"He does have a bad temperament," the sorceress said. "You'd be wise to do as he says."

"Leave us alone…" Mara thrust a dagger out at the woman.

The sorcerers broke into laughter, wide smiles stretching across their faces, as if they were in pain.

"You expect us to be scared of a little mouse with a dagger?" Calasar said.

Talis tried to remember what he'd done to cast the fire spell. If he could only cast it again. He raised his hands towards Calasar, then stopped. Calasar had a long, nasty scar that stretched across his face. When he grinned, it was more like a snarl. Talis knew he didn't stand a chance of defeating them.

"If you're thinking of casting a spell, beware," the woman said. "He'll make it very painful for you. You'll stay alive, and yet Master Calasar has an amazing knack for delivering excruciating torture, especially to the toenails and fingernails. Imagine! An electrical spell that only inflicts pain to the tips of your fingers and to your stubby little mouse toes. Simply genius, don't you think?"

Mara lowered her dagger in defeat, and cast a wary glance at Calasar.

"I won't hurt him…if he behaves." Calasar grabbed Talis by the wrist. In a flash of brilliant light, the sorcerer summoned a dark and shimmering magical portal. "Inside you go. Tell your friend goodbye, for it's likely the last time you'll ever see her."

"No!" Mara shouted, and grasped the blue amulet hanging around her neck. "Hear me, Goddess Nestria, my plea is simple and my heart pure. Prevent these dark ones from taking my friend."

Calasar turned and laughed. "The little mouse begs to the Goddess of the Sky? As if Nestria would ever hear a mouse's plea? Sooner Zagros would take you."

At the name of the Lord of the Underworld, low rumblings and hissings could be heard throughout the crypts, as if all the dead masters of the Order complained in unison. Talis and Mara and the sorcerers turned to face the sound. A rushing wind struck their faces, a hot wind, smelling of pine and storm. Dust also came, blasting their eyes, and Talis fell to his knees, pinching his eyes shut, trying to make tears to clear his vision. But the wind only increased, striking so fiercely that the stones of the mausoleum made an awful splintering crack.

"Who dares violate my house of rest?" a high, nasally voice boomed nearby. Talis could hear a loud stirring inside the mausoleum, as if the champion were waking from a long slumber.

"It sounds as if the Goddess has heard this little mouse's plea after all," Mara said, her eyes filled with righteous fury.

"The dead obey Calasar," the woman said, her voice unconvinced. "He's mastered the shadow and the necrotic arts."

"Including one such as I?" A shriveled, pasty mess of a mummified man stumbled out of the mausoleum, wearing a ring mail coat and leggings of some dull silver alloy. He coughed and vile dust spewed from his lungs, the stench of spoiled flesh and organs. He lifted a curved blade with great difficulty, and stared along its battle-worn edge. Sighing, the man growled a deep, powerful growl, as if angry at his condition. Soon the withered and dried flesh under his skin wiggled to life, filling his body with youth once again. His bald flaky scalp turned ruddy and chestnut hair spilled down to his shoulders. And yet a scar on his neck, present in death, remained.

Calasar strode up to the champion, stopped, and stared up at the inscription. "Master Baribariso, I presume?"

The champion scowled at nowhere in particular, flourished his sword, and allowed it to slice cleanly through Calasar's neck. Master Baribariso grunted, ignoring the head that gurgled on the ground, blood gushing from its mouth.

"And you, my pet?" he said, and stared tenderly at the woman.

She shrieked, and chose instead to flee inside the magical portal, which closed up behind her in a vast whooshing sound.

Master Baribariso sniffed and glanced around. "Such cowards exist in this time. Who has summoned me?"

Mara shrunk back, inviting the champion's stare.

"Little one, be not afraid... I won't harm you." Master Baribariso sheathed his sword, and with a long sigh, stretched his spine. "I am tired from my long sleep. It pains me to find myself back in mortal flesh. The Fair Seas of the Underworld were so kind to me."

"Have you seen my brother?" Talis said, his voice trembling. "A stout young man, Xhan Storm."

"Ah, names and titles and grand positions...none are of importance in the Underworld." He touched his head, as if trying to remember something. "I had a name once, before the shroud of death washed my memory clean. What was it now?"

"Master Baribariso—"

"Yes! That's it, what a grand name. Now it's all coming back." The champion placed a finger on his forehead, as if trying to remember. "There is more, so much more. Oh! And I have a message for you—the both of you. Today is a day of war and mourning. Mothers are weeping above in the City of Naru." He tapped his head, and reached out his hand, as if grasping something from the sky. A shimmering mist appeared and from within it he withdrew a circular map case with a golden clasp, shaped in the image of the sun.

"What is that?" Mara said, her voice suddenly excited.

"This is not for you, and yet it pertains to you, as you are connected to the grand scheme." The Master handed Talis the map case. "Within lies the ancient Surineda Map, spoken of in legend, hidden by the Goddess Nestria until the time when the world needs the light to balance out the darkness."

"Master Holoron spoke of this map." Talis stared at the case. "Is this real or a waking dream? Have I dreamed all this—"

"This is no dream, young master. Soon your city will ask things of you that bear a heavy burden. You must leave your city...."

"Leave Naru?" Talis said.

The champion nodded, and peered into Talis's eyes. "You must leave all this behind and follow the noble path, the warrior's path. When you open the map case, the Surineda Map will point you to your destination. And you must obey, or this world will fall...fall into endless darkness."

"But how can I leave now? Now that we're at war?"

"You will find a way." Master Baribariso's eyes shone with a golden light. "I feel the lure of the Immortals pulling me. I have answered the call of the Goddess, left the comfort of the Fair Seas, and now a new way opens before me. I wonder..."

A silver and gold portal appeared in the darkness of the crypts, and the champion disappeared inside.

9

The Sej Elders

Under twilight's soft haze, the smoking city of Naru looked like an injured dog licking its wounds. Talis surveyed the damage, staring out over the city from the deck outside his bedroom loft. Smoldering fires here and there, broken towers, cracks in the temple dome, many houses and buildings in ruin. But considering the scope of the attack, the damage was less than he'd expected. And their wizards did successfully repel the invaders.

But would they survive the next attack? Perhaps with an army at the gates and ground support for the sorcerers?

He yawned, surprised that he'd slept all day after finally crawling to bed early in the morning hours after the attack. In his hands he held the golden map case, given to him by the champion in the crypts. *But really it was the Goddess Nestria herself that gave the gift,* he thought. Why would a Goddess care for the concerns of a mortal boy?

Unable to dare open the case, he held it as if it were a coiled serpent waiting to strike. As if it might bring ruin to his life. Where would the Surineda Map lead him? An ache in his gut told him it would be far away, far from his home, far from the coming battle with the Jiserian Empire. For he knew they would return again with a much stronger force. That was the way kings and emperors acted.

Would the map even help make a difference? And could he make it back in time to help? Talis heard soft footfalls behind him. He tensed, but relaxed as he recognized Mara's steps.

"You're improving at stealth," he said. "But I still knew it was you."

"How could you tell?" Mara jumped on his back and landed a kiss on his neck. "You're not supposed to hear me coming, you're supposed to be surprised."

"I'm trained to listen to you." Talis flipped her around, and stopped, gaping at her painted pretty face and curled hair. "What happened to you?"

Mara shrugged, and giggled at his no doubt confused face. "Mother's determined to marry me off to another nobleman's son. After we won the Blood Dagger, she's agreed to let me reject the warthog, but then she got the idea for me to marry the son of the Earl of Shanick. I hate that woman. Our city is under attack and all she can think about is getting me married? And now she's insisted I get all done up like this and meet with his parents...."

"But you're here...aren't you going to be in trouble?"

"Whatever... I'm not marrying him and I'm not interested in meeting his stupid old parents."

Talis chuckled. "How did you get away?"

"Now that's a story. They locked me in the fourth floor servant quarters."

"And you escaped out the window and climbed all the way down?"

"I eluded several guardsmen and servants at the front."

Mara's face turned serious all of a sudden. "But listen, I didn't come here for fun. You've got to go to the Sej Elders and show them the Surineda Map."

"I'm not going yet—"

"Have you even bothered opening it?" She scowled. "You haven't, have you? Give it to me."

"I've been sleeping all day. No...listen, I'm supposed to open it. The champion gave it to me."

"Then what are you waiting for? Stop sleeping all the time..." She winked at him and prodded his shoulder with a finger. "Hurry up all ready."

Of course he knew she was right... He glanced at the map case and a feeling a dread twisted in his stomach. What might the map reveal to him? Somehow he realized the reason for his delay in opening the map was the promise of tearing him away from Naru and his family, and pulling him away from Mara as well. He didn't want to find himself away from her.

Finally, at her insisting eyes, he grabbed the case and twisted open the latch. Inside, the coiled parchment glowed with a faint golden light. He withdrew the map, and felt a radiant heat slither up his arms until his entire body became radiated with heat. *This really is from the Goddess,* Talis thought.

A sudden wave of sleepiness washed over him and his eyes closed in response. *Where am I?* Talis thought, and scanned around an empty, expansive world of golden light. Past a shimmering mist he saw a shape appear. A beautiful, luminescent woman with golden, flowing hair observed him, as if measuring his worth. After she seemed satisfied, and she nodded and disappeared into the mist.

Talis woke with a lurching start. His heart was pounding and his palms were flushed and hot.

"What happened to you?" Mara said, her eyes flared in concern.

"I think I just saw the Goddess of the Sun, the Goddess Nacrea."

"You had a vision of the Goddess?"

Talis caught Mara's wondering expression, and he nodded his head at the map. It was sealed with a waxy stamp, marked with an illustration of the sun. He glanced at Mara's urging eyes. Again he touched the map and the heat surged again. This time he broke the seal and the map released a hissing sound like a spitting snake.

As he unfurled the map, a warm, golden light spilled out from within, revealing the shimmering landmass of the continent Talis was familiar with, as well as other areas unknown: a large snowy island to the north, scattered islands off to the west with one long, spindly island running alongside, and far to the east, beyond the city of Khael, was a lush, tropical island. When he stared at that island, he could feel warm sunlight flowing through his veins. That was it, the island... They had to travel to that island.

Mara seemed to have followed his gaze, for she pointed at the spot where his eyes were fixed. "Is that where we're going?"

"I think so... I feel something strong there. I never knew such islands existed—"

"I've seen a map in Master Holoron's library showing the western islands...but not this one." Her finger ran along the map, and she winced as if noticing the heat that emanated from within.

"Be careful, there's heat locked inside. The power of Light Magic is stored within...."

"You have to tell the Elders about the map. Don't shake your head, you have to do it! Last night was only the first attack... The next time will be worse."

Next time. Talis felt the hairs along the back of his neck prickle in pain. He pictured the dark sorcerers raining shadows and fire and lightning bolts down on the city. And that was only an aerial attack. If the Jiserian ground forces came here with siege machines and armies of undead, what would be left of their city? Or could the map help them to win in their fight against the Jiserian Empire? He had to believe it could.

"Just take the map to them—the Sej Elders will listen—take it at once." Mara shoved her hands on her hips, as if daring him to think otherwise.

Talis bowed his head, and gave in. She was right. Although he had never been to the Sej Elder chambers, he always wondered what it would be like to finally set foot inside. His father was the leading member of the Elders, but had refused Talis entry until he came of age. He was about to head downstairs when he stopped, realizing the problem. There was no way they'd let him inside. Especially now that the Elders were debating about how to best respond to the Jiserian threat.

"Who's going to listen to us…we're just kids." Talis glanced at Mara. "Even if we went, they won't let us in. It's forbidden."

"Find a way around… Let's sneak inside." Mara's eyes glittered dangerously.

"The entrance is heavily guarded by multiple soldiers and wizards and at different levels. Especially now that we're at war. And my father isn't popular these days. He's always talking about how his seat at the head of the Elders is at risk. If I did something crazy like trying to break in and see them, he'd be furious."

"Then talk to Master Viridian."

"He's in chambers with them also! We should just wait for them outside."

"Wait? Do you think we have time to wait?" Her faced fumed and her eyes narrowed. "This is directly related to the war. Whether we like it or not we're part of the conflict now. This could mean everything to our struggle!"

"You're right, this is important to the war. I think we just need a better plan, ok?" He sighed and caught her softening eyes. "Let's talk on the way there. Maybe we'll get an idea."

They snuck out the window and wound their way around the garden and down the cobblestone street, chatting at random along the way. Mara always talked on and on when she was agitated and nervous. He couldn't help but smile to see her all worked up like that. After a short walk they reached the building where two burly guards stood at attention outside the tall gate surrounding the Sej Elders Chambers. More soldiers marched out front. The city was priming itself for war.

"State your own business," The larger guard's frown changed to panic at Talis approached.

"Watch what you say," Mara said, and glowered at the guard. "Do you know who you're speaking to?"

"I'm sorry, Your Royal Highness." The guard bowed, and apologized for his poor eyesight.

"That's all right, the gods do favor the young and curse the old." Mara smirked at the old soldier. "Now be a good guard and go fetch us the runner, we demand an audience with the Elders."

"Demand an audience?" the other guard said, "but they're in an urgent war counsel meeting now."

"This is *urgent*…you do remember we've been attacked? He's carrying something very important that the Elders need to see—"

"I understand, I do, miss. If you just kindly leave it with me, I'll make sure they get it."

"In person." Talis scowled. "I need to deliver it to the Elders in person."

"Need to deliver what?" Master Jai said, a teacher at the Order of the Dawn. He pulled a black cowl off his head and sauntered over to them.

"Good evening, Master Jai," the guard said.

The Master waved the guard away. "Yes, well, what is this all about, young master Talis? What do you need to deliver to your father? Speak."

"I carry a sacred map of utmost importance to our struggle, it was given to me— I cannot speak more now, it must be spoken only to the Elders."

"Then come inside now." He glanced at Mara. "I'm afraid you'll have to wait outside, Your Royal Highness. Your parents would be furious to see you associating with young Talis. I cannot get involved in Royal House politics."

Mara was about to speak when Master Jai raised a finger, as if ending all conversion. He motioned Talis inside through the gates and led him into a long corridor. Talis glanced back at Mara. She had already turned and was stomping sullenly away.

The entrance to the chambers wasn't like he'd expected. A worn sandstone archway and a rough oak door supported by iron slats. Inside, the damp air smelled of mold and rot. A runner greeted them, carrying a lantern as he led them further inside. They marched down a long, dark hallway then followed stone steps sinking even deeper. Wavering shadows bounced along the glistening ceiling. Talis could feel his skin flush, hot with anticipation for how his father might react.

The runner rapped three times on a heavy, oaken door. Another guard opened it and peered through. He waved them inside once he recognized Master Jai. Four more guards stood at attention along a waiting corridor, and glanced suspiciously at Talis. Once Master Jai had set his hand on Talis's shoulder, leading him on, they looked away. Finally, the runner opened a set of doors, crafted of intricately carved mahogany. He called out in a nasally, high-pitched voice.

"Announcing Master Jai Nomellius, and young Talis Storm."

Talis's heart fluttered as he glimpsed his father sitting at the head of an enormous table surrounded by the other thirteen Elders. Hundreds of candles lined the stone walls, casting inky, flickering shadows on their faces. Grave expressions, as if they'd been told of a loved one's death. They were staring at Talis like they were irritated that he was here. His father glared at him, a look of absolute incredulity on his face. Talis felt like he'd made a mistake coming here tonight.

"Master Jai, what's the nature of this? Why have you brought my son here?" Garen Storm itched his shoulder.

The door slammed shut behind them and a soldier bolted the door. Talis felt trapped, deep in this underground maze. He noticed four champions standing uneasily at each corner of the room, studying at him as if taking in a new threat.

"Your son holds something in his hands, something he claims that only the Elders can see."

"What is that...a map case?" Elder Vellar Lei, Mara's father, leaned forward, his beady, sunken eyes staring at the map. His wrinkled lips moved as if chewing on his own tongue.

Talis cleared his parched throat, and withered from all the intense stares.

"Speak up, boy." His father scowled, and tapped the table impatiently.

"Last night we were attacked—"

"What's inside the map case?" Elder Vellar boomed, "we don't have time for stories."

"Let the boy speak." Master Viridian stood. "I sense something powerful in his hands. Let him tell his story."

"As I was saying, last night…while on the temple walls, we were attacked. M—" Talis stopped himself from saying Mara's name. "Attacked by sorcerers, one came directly at me, and chased us to the Crypts."

"The Crypts? Whatever for?" Elder Vellar said, a puzzled expression on his face.

"For the last time, let him speak!"

Talis glanced nervously around. "Trapped we were…in the Crypts…there were two sorcerers. One tried to take me through a shimmering portal. I thought I was doomed. Mara"—Talis coughed, latching eyes with Elder Vellar's cold stare—"she prayed to the Goddess Nestria, and the Goddess heard her cry. A fallen champion, Master Baribariso, he rose to life, summoned by the Goddess, and slew the sorcerer."

"*The* Legendary Master Baribariso who rests in the Crypts?" Master Holoron said, his head shaking in disbelief.

"No longer. He slumbers in the Crypts no more. He has gone to join the Immortals…" Talis stared at

Holoron, and flicked his hand towards the sky. "Here, in my hands, I hold his gift… Before the champion left, he gave me this, saying the Goddess Nestria hid this for a time like this, a time where the world needs the power of the Goddess Nacrea."

"Is it true? Do you hold in your hands the Surineda Map?" Holoron said, rising to his feet.

Talis nodded at the Elders as they stared in surprise at the map case. He felt an anxious excitement as he twisted open the latch. The Elders gasped as Talis unrolled the map and displayed it to them all. In that instant, the candles were extinguished and the map shone in the darkness. He experienced a wave of dizziness as the map blazed. He could see flickering fragments of the Goddess's face, an island forgotten by time, forgotten by civilization, and a wrinkled face veiled by smoldering fumes, a broken city nestled in a graveyard.

A snapped finger caused flame to return to the candles, revealing a deathly pallor on the Elders' faces. They had seen it too. The vision.

"Behold!" Master Viridian said, "the Surineda Map. Spoken of in legend, and here before us now. Given by the Goddess for the time when needed most."

"I saw the Goddess Nacrea!" shouted an Elder.

"An strange and terrible island."

"A city covered in ash, the temple shattered and in ruins—"

"No the temple stands! I saw it!" shouted another. "You saw the old temple. I saw the true one, in a grove, hidden away. The doorway to it...unseen."

Master Viridian raised his arms, standing. "Now, now, quiet, now. We all saw different visions, that is clear enough. For each the Goddess chose to reveal a different vision. What is certain is the map is true. We must obey its commands." He stared at Talis, as if expecting him to continue.

"The champion of Naru, Master Baribariso, told me I must leave Naru and follow the map where it leads."

"You? You are but a boy. Why would the Goddess choose you?" Master Vellar scoffed.

"He's *my* boy! Refrain from insulting him." Garen Storm rose to his feet, towering over Master Vellar. "The gods have spoken to us. If we listen and obey we'll live and thrive and survive this abominable war with the Jiserians. If we deny them—as a fool would— we deny ourselves. Well, Elders? What say you?"

Regent Balmarr Merillia, King of Naru, shadow Elder at the table, stood finally and raised a white-gloved hand. "We'll assemble a force, a force greater than anyone has ever seen, and task this force with delivering the boy to the destination the map directs. We'll spare no gold, and charge the best in our land with success. Swordsmen, pikemen, rangers—be a foe to our enemies and those that dare stand in the way. We will succeed! The gods have spoken. They stand on our side."

Master Vellar snorted. "Have you forgotten about the Jiserians, Regent Merillia? Send this force out to the ends of the earth, while they ravage our homeland?"

"We can spare a party of swordsmen to protect the expedition," said Garen Storm. "From *each* of the Royal Houses." He glanced shrewdly around the table.

"Then it's settled," Regent Merillia said, and he turned and faced Talis. "Leave us now—to settle the details. Time is of utmost importance. I say the party must leave before daybreak tomorrow."

The other Elders voiced "ayes" in agreement. Talis bowed, and shuffled out of the chambers. Leave Naru tomorrow? Leave his home and family, and perhaps never return…tomorrow?

10

The Fire Sword

After Talis left the Sej Elder chambers, he searched around the city for Mara but couldn't find her anywhere. He finally gave up and returned home at twilight, disappointed that she couldn't talk to her. His house was dark and warm, and shadows danced along the walls. Mother sat by the fire, knitting a wool scarf, and Father glanced at Talis and sighed, shifting uncomfortably in his chair.

"Where have you been all this time? Looking for that Lei girl?"

"It was her prayer that summoned the champion. The Goddess Nestria heard her."

"Well her father has her locked up good now. You saw his face when you mentioned his daughter's name. Vellar just about threw a fit." Garen chuckled, as if amused at his own private joke. "Serves him right, I suppose. She's a wild one, that girl. Lady Malvia faces an impossible task of containing her."

"You used to be friends with Mara's mother?" As soon as Talis said it, he knew it was the wrong thing to say. His father's face darkened, brooding on some old wound. Mother didn't even glance at his comment.

Father sniffed, lifting his head as if leaving everything unpleasant behind. "Tomorrow then, it's all settled. Do you require help from the servants on packing for the voyage? I imagine traveling lightly is the best way to go."

Talis noticed the color drain from his mother's face as Father talked. Wrinkles formed hard crevices on her forehead, and her breath went shallow. She exhaled, her body rigid, and her eyes glazed over as she stared at the flames.

After a long silence, she whispered, "Where is my son going?"

Talis grimaced as his mother lowered her head in a gesture of defeat.

"Far away, dear...north across the desert, past the barren lands, to an island, I suppose. Not on any of our maps, but there nonetheless."

"But he's so young." Her hands shook, then she calmed herself and put down her knitting.

"He'll be protected by our soldiers." Garen narrowed his eyes at Talis, and puffed on a carved, wooden pipe. "Now then, go on, rest awaits you. We'll see to everything, just you see."

Talis turned and shuffled off, lost in thought. Would they really be protected by their soldiers, out there in the vast Nalgoran Desert and the cold lands of the north? And how could he leave without Mara? There had to be a way to see her....

Early the next morning, before any light touched the sky, Talis stared out his window. A hard lump clenched his stomach as he thought of leaving home for the first time. He held the map case, and still sensed the warmth inside. *The heat that separates and tears you apart from your home,* thought Talis. Would he make it back safe? Or even if he did make it back alive, would there even be a home to come back to?

Downstairs, he caught sight of his mother packing food for his journey. He gazed at his mother's face, memorizing every curve and line. He hoped that she'd be all right. As if she knew exactly what he was feeling, she reached out and hugged him, and choked back the tears.

"Nothing will keep us apart for long... You'll come back to us, I feel it in my bones." The weight of her words made him even sadder to leave.

His father ambled down the hallway, carrying something wrapped in silk. "I've something for you, son. I'd hope to give this to you when you came of age. It will prove valuable on your journey...."

His father handed him a sheathed short sword.

Talis withdrew the sword, and gaped at the red-tinged steel with ghost patterns and smoky lines running along the blade. A tremendous weight rushed up his arm from the sword, as if imbued with some terrific power. He tensed his arm and winced. Father was really giving him this treasure? The sheath was made of blackened leather, and elaborate swirling patterns ran down the spine, with silver studs lining the edge. Talis gasped. It was immaculate. Why would Father give him such a priceless gift?

"This...this sword is for me?" He gazed at the ruby-studded hilt, a puma's face with ruby eyes shaping the hilt's edge.

"It's the finest sword in Naru." Father narrowed his eyes at the expression on Talis's face. "What is it, what are you feeling?"

"I'm not sure," Talis stammered, fighting the power.

His father's eyes sparkled. "You're sensing the power within the sword—"

"It's magical?" What did his father know of such things? He was a man of commerce and trade.

"The magical gift runs deep in our family history." Father took the sword from Talis and raised it to the firelight. "This is no regular sword...it possesses great power. The red color is not from blood, there's Fire Magic within." Fire Magic...Master Viridian said his element was fire, Talis thought.

Father returned the sword, and Talis stared at him, tears welling in his eyes. "I never imagined I'd have a treasure like this."

"Take care of the sword, it's part of you now. There's an old saying, 'As the bearer wields, so he holds his life in his hands.' So beware, I don't give you the sword lightly."

"Thank you, Father." Talis reached out and shook his hand, still not believing Father had entrusted such a gift to him.

"Are you truly willing to embark on such an important mission?"

It was the question Talis had been waiting to hear from his father for many years. A chance to prove himself and make him proud. Of course he'd go; of course he'd do anything to protect Naru and his family. This adventure was what he'd been dreaming about his whole life.

He simply gazed into his father's eyes and said, "I am."

"Good, don't fail to make me proud, son. Much rests on your shoulders."

Talis embraced his mother again, then stepped out into the dimly lit streets. Down through the upper and lower city and out past the northern gates, he followed a soldier that led him north until they reached the first traces of the Nalgoran Desert. Torches illuminated the area where men loaded supplies onto the horses. He was really leaving. There was no going back now.

He stared back at the city. The massive stone walls were painted in a surreal orange glow from the torches. Those ancient walls, designed by men of science and magic to withstand the strongest physical and magical attacks. Over twenty feet thick, those walls scintillated with the power of warding runes.

But as he studied them, a cruel thought struck him. *Will those walls hold until I return?*

Talis turned north and gazed at the faint glow lining the horizon. A meteor flared across the field of stars. He shivered at the cold and looked up at the sky, wondering what was out there. He didn't feel alone when he looked at the stars, but tonight, and for how long he didn't know, he would be alone. He didn't even get to say goodbye to Mara. Just like that, he was leaving.

"Star gazing?" Rikar swaggered over and covered his head with a black hood. "The desert holds a chill."

"What are you doing here?"

"What? Your father didn't tell you?" Rikar laughed. "I suppose Master Viridian failed to mention that Nikulo and me are coming. Did you honestly think they'd leave the task all up to you?"

"The map was given to me."

"A mistake. Must have meant to give it to me instead. Maybe out in the desert, that *mistake* will be corrected." Rikar turned and strode away, humming a dark tune, a song of jealousy and the fate of the blade. Why did the Elders invite them? Talis felt his face flush as he clenched his hands. The politics of the Royal Houses had to be involved....

The men preparing the horses finished cinching down the packs, whistled, and waved everyone over. The soldiers came first. Talis recognized a few men and women from his father's company. He strode over to the horses, admiring their fine sheen. Talis stroked his mare's grey mane and inspected the packs. Scanning the horizon, he felt a presence out to the northwest. Like a hand searching the desert.

Something was out there.

Talis turned as Nikulo waddled towards the party, wiggling his fingers in his pockets.

"Did I miss anything exciting?" He scanned around. His eyes had a playful, mischievous look.

"Ah, good company for the long ride." Rikar clasped hands with Nikulo. "A shame about all the lovely ladies we'll be leaving behind."

Nikulo yawned and covered his mouth. "Ladies you say? Look here, they've invited a girl on the expedition."

"A girl with an ugly face," Rikar said, and flicked a pebble at Talis.

Talis ignored the jape, and instead pictured his sword slicing through Rikar's armor at the Blood Dagger competition. He grinned and turned away.

Master Jarvis Numerian tromped over to the group, his long black hair swinging back and forth. He glared at them. "Who invited you?"

Talis swallowed and glanced around. "The Elders—"

"Am I to play wet nurse to these saplings?" Master Jarvis ignored Talis, and scowled at Rikar and Nikulo.

"Will you change our diapers too?" Nikulo said, grinning.

Jarvis grunted and scraped a boot against the sand. "This isn't the practice arena. You'll have no healer to save you from your own stupidity."

"Nikulo knows the art of healing," Rikar said. "We'll be fine on our own."

"We'll see about that." Jarvis gestured at Talis. "So you're supposedly the one leading this little jaunt into the northlands? A boy and his magical map?"

"He claims the gods gave him—"

"Was I talking to you?" Jarvis scowled at Rikar, then faced Talis. "Well then, what are you waiting for, lead on…"

The wind shifted and came up from the south, a warm wind, blowing against their backs as they faced north. Talis mounted and gazed at the shimmering horizon. He withdrew the Surineda Map, allowing it to light the dark way. The path was clear, but the way unsettling. Something was waiting for them.

11

The Nalgoran Desert

The cold wind blew unceasingly from the north: a violent wind, a merciless wind, a wind that crept inside your ears and pressed hard against the back of your neck. The desert sands swirled, and left a lingering haze in the air. Talis lifted his head and stared. The afternoon sun blurred over the horizon. The day had turned sour, and now a sand storm pelted them mercilessly.

He bent over his horse and clung to the reins, searching the horizon for signs of life. The journey across the desert was unlike anything he'd experienced. The wind left him feeling exhilarated and exhausted at the same time. They'd ridden long and hard that day, the desert growing colder each mile as the party rode north over the white sands. The eyes of the soldiers looked hard and irritated, as if angry that they'd been commanded on the journey.

Talis rode up to Jarvis. "When will we make camp for the day?" He could barely stay on his horse and his tailbone was numb.

"Quit complaining. Did you think your mama was coming?" Jarvis kicked his horse, and trotted ahead.

An hour after twilight, the storm cleared and the party reached a ghostly oasis, dimly lit under the four moon sisters. The soldiers slumped off their horses, jostling around and joking with each other. Jarvis grunted and ordered them to collect wood and start a fire. The party bustled about, unloading supplies from the horses and setting up camp.

Talis was starving and couldn't wait for the soldiers to cook dinner. He rummaged through his packs and found a bag of dried meat. He smiled and thanked the gods for giving him such a wonderful mother. He ate a few pieces until his stomach stopped complaining.

"What's this?" Jarvis said, eying the dried meat. "No acting the noble brat out here with the troops hard at work. Pull your own weight… Do something useful like starting a fire."

Withering from the harsh words, Talis nodded and marched over to where several soldiers were assembling wood for the fire. The men regarded him suspiciously, but moved away as Talis raised his hands at the wood, attempting to cast Fire Magic again.

But before he even had a chance to try, a spidering flame illuminated the dark night and engulfed the wood in a whoosh. The magic disappeared, leaving only the brightly burning campfire.

"Can't even cast a simple flame to start a fire?" Rikar said, his voice filled with contempt. He emerged from the shadows, chuckling with Nikulo.

"That's what I was about to do..." Talis muttered.

"No, what he was about to do was to lose control of magic and kill himself and everyone else around him!" Rikar said, his face suddenly turning wrathful. Talis knew he was still furious at him over Cassis's death.

The soldiers went silent, staring at Rikar and Talis like they were about to fight. Some even stepped back into the shadows, as if wary of wizard duels.

"I ask you to start a fire, not start a fight!" Master Jarvis marched up and glared at them. "Now do something useful...preferably in difference places, do you hear me?"

Talis nodded, and Rikar skulked off towards his horse, Nikulo trailing gloomily.

"And did I give permission for the rest of you to just stand there gaping at these fools?" Jarvis shouted.

The soldiers grunted and went back to their work, setting up a cooking pot over the fire and preparing dinner. Talis helped them unload the food bags and one of the soldiers thanked him and said they could do the rest.

After eating dinner, Talis seized a woolen blanket and retreated to a place behind several bushes, a place well shielded from the northern wind. He lay down and thought about the past week, and all the strange things that had happened. Had it only been two days since the Jiserians had attacked Naru? And where was Mara now, locked up someplace in the Lei mansion, probably furious at her parents? He realized just how much he missed her.

Talis let his thoughts drift away, and he stared at the stars flickering in the sky. He closed his eyes and listened to the soft sounds of the sand shifting across the desert, and soon fell asleep.

A rustling sound in the bushes woke him with a start. He tensed and found himself completely awake in an instant. When the sound came closer, Talis gripped his short sword, feeling the fire crawl into his pounding chest.

"It's me," Mara whispered, holding her hand out to stop him. "Put your sword away."

"What? Mara? But...how in the name of the gods did you get here?"

"Can't you see I'm in disguise?" She pulled her hood down and grinned. "Proper soldier of House Lei... Did you miss me?"

"Of course! I can't believe you escaped from your father. Everyone said he had locked you away."

"He did...but he doesn't know that I can pick all the locks in the house. I sneaked out in the middle of the night while everyone was sleeping...including the guard at the front gate."

"Good secret to keep." Talis grinned, and moved aside to let her sit. "I'm really glad you came—"

"Somebody had to keep you from getting yourself killed. When I heard Rikar and Nikulo were selected for the party, I was furious. I couldn't let you go alone...especially not with grumpy Master Jarvis and those two fools...."

"Did you eat?"

Mara shrugged, and tossed him a mischievous look. "I packed chocolate and sweet bread."

"That's not food!"

"I didn't want Rikar or Nikulo or Master Jarvis to recognize me by the fire..."

"Here, have some dried meat. My mother packed it this morning."

Mara nibbled on the edges. "This is delicious... You know, I really love your mother's food. Why can't

I have your mother? Mine never cooks. Can we swap?"

"Not in a million years," Talis said.

They huddled close to keep warm, and went quiet for a while, listening to the droning sounds of insects in the oasis. Talis's mood darkened, knowing that sooner or later someone would recognize Mara. "But what are we going to do when they find that you're here? You know they will, eventually."

"Worry about that when the time comes." Mara lay next to him, and he pulled the blanket over them, and together they stared at the stars. Twin meteors shot across the black sky, and sent a pulsing thrill shooting through his heart. Mara was really here with him… For the first time since leaving on the trip, hope blossomed in his heart.

After three grueling days journeying north through the desert, Talis stared out across a stormy horizon, wishing they could finally leave this bleak place. How far was it to the northlands? Jarvis had refused to answer his questions all day. They'd stopped to rest in a gully underneath a massive sand dune. Talis studied the laughing eyes of the soldiers around him and wondered what was going on.

Rikar was entertaining the soldiers, again, telling crude jokes and making fun of people in Naru. But mostly, he said things at Talis's expense. He told stories about Xhan, Talis's older brother, and what a tremendous fighter Xhan had been (as opposed to Talis). It didn't matter that Talis had beat Rikar in the Blood Dagger competition, Rikar always chose to tell stories about older fights in which Talis had lost. Rikar whispered something into a younger soldier's ear, and they both scoffed and shook their heads at Talis.

Could the expedition get any worse? Talis wished he'd gotten to know his father's men, as they seemed to have the same challenging attitude towards him that his father had had for all these years. Especially the younger ones.

Mara kept quiet, keeping her face covered in disguise; she wasn't about to get escorted back to Naru by one of the soldiers. Talis caught her gripping her dagger as Rikar was deep in a story ridiculing Talis. This wasn't easy for her either.

Talis opened a pack and withdrew more dried meat from his dwindling supplies. He was getting sick of dried pork and dried beef. With the wind and storm as strong as it was, they didn't even attempt to start a fire. He knew he couldn't expect much in the way of variety on the expedition, especially the farther they went north and the colder it got. But still he missed the ovens of Naru filled with sweet bread and pies, dumpling soup from Fiskar's Market, and most of all, his mother's cooking.

But after an hour or so of waiting out the storm, the wind slowed and the clouds dissipated. An eerie calm possessed the desert as the soldiers stared around in wonder. One of the soldiers let out a shrill whistle, and Talis turned and noticed that the others behind him were staring at the western horizon.

"Raiders," shouted Jarvis.

Talis squinted at the horizon and spotted a dust cloud far off in the distance swirling towards them.

"Prepare to ride!" Jarvis yelled, and charged around his men. They gathered their gear and mounted up. "Battle formation, but keep it loose and fast, I'd rather not engage whoever is out there." *Or whatever is out there,* Talis thought.

Talis scrambled onto his horse and rode after them, the wind stinging his face as they sped north. The horses of Naru were famous across the western world. Bred for speed and endurance, the thoroughbreds selected for the expedition were among the finest champions of Naru. But as Talis glanced back, whoever was chasing them rode like demons....

An inky-black sandstorm swirled behind the group that chased them, the fringes of which reached up to the zenith. The storm rose higher and higher as they gained on them, until it seemed that the darkness would blot out the sky. White uniforms against the black sky. The Jiserian army.

The enemy soldiers on horseback didn't travel alone. A hundred feet in the air behind them flew three figures in blood-red cloaks. Shadow tendrils lapped at their legs, shrouding their feet. Outstretched hands created the power of the storm. Talis watched as the figure on the left dove from the sky and brought a spiraling arm down, a black lance of shadow and sand. The storm aimed directly at Talis and his group. How could the Jiserians know that they were out here?

His horse reared, spooked by the fury of the elemental assault. Talis stopped and gaped at the avalanche of the approaching army. They would die out here. Or be captured and taken as slaves. Or worse, tortured for information.

A few seconds before the spiraling arm struck, it curved inwards and away, sending a blast of cold, sulfuric air washing over them. Talis froze, clearly seeing the Jiserian soldiers now. They weren't human. At least not anymore. The soldiers and horses were all bone and rotting flesh. Swirling red and gold orbs blazed in their eye sockets. An undead army had been sent to slay them.

Talis glanced up at the figures in the sky. Necromancers. He gripped his short sword and felt the heat hurtle up through his hand and race down his spine.

Jarvis rode up to the front, as if he could stop the overwhelming force. "Stay back!" The master swordsman brandished his great two-handed sword and bellowed at the enemy army.

The undead soldiers raised swords and axes and halberds as they charged them, leaving a cloud of dust in their wake. They rode in a twin blade formation, splitting before they reached the party. Circling, the undead soldiers paused and leered at them.

The lead necromancer flew down from the sky and landed twenty feet away. A writhing pool of shadows swirled in her webbed hand. "You will surrender." She extended a palm towards Jarvis. Talis had never seen such a terror before. Waves of shadowy mist billowed from her figure and light spilled in from above and illuminated the mist. Her eyes were radiant and cruel, yet her face looked like a child.

"Go to hell," shouted Jarvis, and raised his sword.

The woman giggled in delight and brought her hands together, sending a wave of shadows and light speeding at the soldier. The force slammed into Jarvis, knocking him fifty feet back onto the sand.

"Surrender…or die," the woman said. A devilish smirk appeared on her lips. "You have a choice."

"What do you want with us?" shouted a soldier. "We're a simple scouting party—"

"You lie," the woman hissed, and clenched her face into a twisted scowl. Now, she seemed a thousand years old, with black and pulsing spidery veins running along her neck. She was going to kill them.

Another necromancer with a shaved head landed to the right of the group. "Hand over the boy with the map case."

"I sense the power." The woman strode forward until she was inches from the soldier's face. She sniffed and quickly shifted her inspecting gaze at the soldiers standing near Talis. "A powerful relic is close."

Talis shrank back behind the soldiers, wanting to find a hole to crawl into and disappear forever. They were looking for him. Images of the Crypts and the shimmer portal flashed in his mind. They were trying to take him again.

Some strange power seemed to come over Rikar and he foolishly marched up and stood next to the soldier. The woman had gazed at him as he approached, as if her eyes studied his soul.

"You know of magic." She frowned and shook her head. "Yet you are not the one."

"Deal with me, not the young ones." The soldier stepped in front of Rikar.

"This one talks far too much," the bald necromancer said, and he stretched out his hand and released a flood of demonic faces at the soldier.

The bulky swordsman grabbed his throat, his face turning ashen, neck bulging and throbbing, and he dropped to his knees, face planting into the sand.

"Now the map and the boy, if you please." The woman eyed the other soldiers.

"I have a better idea, let's kill them one by one——"

"Patience, Oren, patience..."

"Talis," Rikar shouted, "you might as well show yourself."

What is he doing? Talis thought. Would Rikar actually be a traitor to his own people? Talis glanced around and noticed the soldiers' eyes fixed forward, refusing to provide any hints to their enemies.

Rikar sighed in resignation and turned his gaze towards Talis. The necromancer followed the direction where Rikar looked, and Talis felt furious at Rikar for giving him away. The feeling of power grew from the sword in his hand, and it built up into an uncontrollable rage, which he fought to suppress with all his power.

"This is the one." The woman flew over to where Talis stood.

Talis withdrew the map case and displayed it to the woman. "Is this what you are looking for?" he said. He used the momentary distraction to advance and plunge the sword into her heart.

A wailing and hissing sound was heard as the necromancer vanished, her body melting into ash. The blood-red cloak wrapped around her floated to the ground.

Half the undead soldiers and horses collapsed around them. Bones clacked against bones, wilting on the sand. The sky cleared. Sunlight rained down on the dark army.

Talis fell to his knees, dizzy from the exertion, blinded by the sudden outpouring of light.

"What did you do that for?" Rikar yelled, and glanced at the glowering faces of the other two necromancers.

Talis laughed madly. He'd killed a necromancer and it felt amazing. Not some wild animal in the swamplands. The most feared opponent on the battlefield. A Jiserian necromancer.

After a brief moment of sunlight, darkness once again rained down. This time it came with a fog so thick it suffocated all visibility. Talis heard a moan that sounded like a soldier being struck. Mara screamed. The sound of steel shattering bone and armor.

"Mara!" he shouted, panicked at the sound of her scream and the shattering armor. A deep, booming roar echoed over the sand, as if the fog itself was the source of all the strikes.

Turning, he charged through the mist towards Mara's voice, hoping to protect her. Out at the edge of the fog, Talis noticed Rikar talking with a shadowy figure. He turned his head towards Talis, as if surprised at being found. The figure disappeared in the fog. What was Rikar doing? Rikar frowned at Talis, a look of malevolence on his face.

A loud, clattering sound interrupted Talis's attention and he swiveled around, spotting four undead warriors striding towards. Their bony faces leered at him, weapons raised in triumph.

The fog lifted in an instant and Talis could see that their party was beaten. At the distraction Rikar charged at an undead soldier, slicing off a head and smashing another apart with a burst of wind from his palm. Talis joined in and severed the other two in half.

But the necromancers, hovering fifty feet off the ground, shot a stream of grey and black particles towards the slain undead and caused them to reassemble back to life. The undead warriors shook their fists above their heads and glowered at Talis and Rikar. Looking around, Talis could see they'd utterly lost. Almost every soldier from the party had been slain or beaten down. The undead surrounded them and the necromancers floated over to gloat over their victory.

"We can't die like this," Talis said, edging closer to Rikar.

"Dying is for quitters," Rikar said, and raised a ruby to his lips. He whispered a name, a name that Talis could barely hear, a name that sounded familiar, like from his nightmares. *Did he say Aurellia?* The jewel glowed red and bits of silver shimmered inside the ruby.

Instantly, it was dark again, so dark that Talis couldn't see his hands.

A rumbling sound could be heard, as if millions of bison charged across a plain. Then a whooshing sound, like when the wind from a storm races through the trees. Brilliant lights pierced the darkness, forming a magical portal filled with shadows and light.

An ancient man, his face distorted and leathered, wore a black hooded robe and stepped through the portal and glanced around, chuckling to himself like he knew some secret joke. He rammed his ruby-tipped staff into the sand. An explosion of red and orange and silver light shot out in all directions and vaporized the undead warriors and horses.

"Be banished to eternal night," he shouted, his voice slow and slurred but powerful, and he aimed his staff at the bald necromancer, and pointed a finger at the other. A rift appeared in the sky and moans and screams of agony from a million dead souls cried out from that rift, as if the sound came from the torments of the Underworld.

The necromancers were pulled (or rather darkness enveloped them) into the rift and they fought and shrieked against the force, but in the end lost the struggle.

And the shadow portal came to the old, grinning man, rushed over him and consumed his body, until he too had disappeared.

The air was clear. The sun was strong. The wind, cold from the north.

12

The Northlands

After the dust settled, Talis could feel the cold dew falling, sending a shiver across his skin. Where had Mara gone? He refused to believe that she was dead. He'd been searching through the bodies, past the bones and fetid flesh of the undead, and watched helpless as soldiers died, exhaling their last breaths. He tried to find Mara, desperate to discover her living face.

Rikar vowed to help, and cast an illumination spell that lit up the night with a shimmering orb. He turned over a dead body, his face revolted at the bloody sight of the hideous face of a former soldier. Talis covered his hand over his mouth and looked away. Gods, the misery of war… Why did the Jiserians have to kill so indiscriminately? They had vastly outnumbered them.

Off a ways from the dead soldiers Talis spotted a trembling lump, and hope swelled in his heart. A survivor? As Talis dashed towards the movement, the lump lifted itself up, and a dirtied face stared around in horror at the destruction.

It was Mara! Talis felt a wave of relief and exhilaration wash over him like a warm summer rain.

"I was so worried…I'd thought you were killed," Talis said, his voice choked with emotion. "Thank the gods you survived." He lifted her up and tenderly embraced her for a long time.

"There's so many soldiers dead," Her whisper was angry and confused. "How could they have died so easily like that?"

Footsteps approached and Talis and Mara turned to face Rikar's surprised face.

"What are you doing here?" Rikar said, his eyes inspecting Mara's armor.

"You think I was going to stay at home and let you all run off on an adventure by yourselves?"

"This isn't some kind of game… You could have been killed," Rikar said. "And your family is probably worried sick about you…."

Mara scoffed. "Forget about them… They want me to marry me off to some stupid Earl's son."

"How did you survive?" Talis asked. She glanced around at all the undead bones lying around.

"When they attacked I knew it was best to pretend I was dead. They attacked the soldiers and ignored me."

"You did the right thing." Talis exhaled and brushed the sand off her clothes.

"Nikulo is probably shivering in his boots, somewhere around here." Rikar squinted, peering out north.

"He was close to me," Mara said, "before Talis attacked the necromancer...."

"Let's find Nikulo and whatever supplies we'll need." Talis rummaged around, checking the bodies for Nikulo. Where were the horses? All their packs, their food and supplies. Even if the threat of attack was over, they'd die out here in the desert without water and a way out and food to survive.

Rikar whistled, calling Talis back to where he was searching with Mara. Mounted on horseback, Nikulo grinned in his cocky way, and held the reins of a second horse.

"Couldn't let these two horses run off," Nikulo said. "I tried to find others..." He stopped when he noticed Mara. "You little she-devil! Who let you come along?"

Mara smiled, flushing a bit. "Nice to see you too."

Nikulo chuckled, and glanced at Talis. "You look terrible, like something sat on your face."

"Well, what happened to you?" Rikar swaggered over to Nikulo's horse. "Weren't you around for the attack?"

"I was trying to stay alive, crawling away the moment they struck."

Rikar scanned the northern horizon. "Looks like we're on our own now, two horses, a few packs, some water, and how many days riding north until we—"

"Get out of this hellhole?" Nikulo frowned. "Two...maybe three days riding. I grabbed this horse and managed to track down the second... Luckily the horses came to me...this one licked me...."

"North? Why would we continue on? The party is demolished...shouldn't we return to Naru?" Rikar said.

"And give up?" Talis sheathed his sword. "I think not. I have the map in my possession. The champion commanded me to go..."

"I'm not saying give up, I'm saying return to Naru and resupply." Rikar frowned, glancing at Nikulo for support.

"If one Jiserian raiding party found us so easily, what's to say another one won't again if we return?"

"Talis has a point," Mara said. "We're lucky we're alive. I say we keep going on."

They had to keep going on, if she returned to Naru, her parents would kill her. And it wasn't luck, it was whomever Rikar had called...that sorcerer saved them, this Aurellia. Who was he, anyway?

"Did you find any other survivors?" Nikulo said.

Rikar frowned. "I'm tired of dead bodies. I went through plenty looking for you."

"I'm going to look...in case there is someone I can heal," Nikulo said, his forehead wrinkled in concern.

Talis rummaged through the mess, trying to find anything useful for the trip. Most of the horses had fled after the attack. Soldiers from his father's armory—who he'd barely known—lying dead on the sand. There were too many to bury.

"Fire will purify the bodies," Rikar said, as if reading his thoughts.

"Wait for Nikulo to check for any survivors." Mara shot Rikar a wrathful look of contempt.

The eastern horizon slowly brightened, awash in the faintest bits of crimson and cobalt, and Talis strode over to meet Nikulo as he waddled towards them. His shoulders sank with a morbid heaviness, as if his grim job had come up fruitless.

He shook his head, and turned to stare at the northern horizon. "We have to keep going."

Rikar faced the mass of bodies, breathing in and out rapidly, the breath of fire. Talis wanted to join in and help, but he couldn't do it. He couldn't bring himself to use magic in this way. The fire danced from body to body, causing the whole mass to explode into flames. The sickly sweet smell of roasted flesh caused Talis to clench his stomach at turn away. He bent over, staring at the light flickering off the sand. He had to get out of there.

They rode north as the sun crept slowly up over the horizon, igniting the desert with a blinding brilliance. As far as he could see there was nothing but swirling sands and rolling dunes, ever changing under the brutal wind. Mara rode with Talis, her hands clenched around his waist as if she was scared of being blown off. It felt so good to have her close to him.

Charting their way with the Surineda Map, they found a small oasis that night, luckily with an old but functioning well. Food was running low. They had enough for maybe another day, and in the oasis they found no game to hunt, just a few palm trees and scraggly bushes. Even a snake would have taste good…if they could've found one.

On the second day they ran out of food. Rikar caught a rattlesnake and roasted it. Tasted like a chewy, tough chicken, but very little meat and after it all, Talis still felt hungry.

The air was colder now, so cold at night it was close to freezing. They were nearing the northlands, close to the Elbegurian Forest and the Turyan River. He'd never felt so tired and sun burnt in his life. If fire was his element, the sun was consuming all the moisture from his body. He felt like he was all dried up. From Mara's tired eyes and deflated expression, he worried whether she had enough water. He had been purposefully drinking less to ensure she'd remain alive.

Late afternoon the next day, after spending a freezing night pressed together between the horses, Talis could see a thin layer of ice covering the last stretch of sand along the northern end of the desert. He let out a cry of joy at the sight of the moisture, and Mara leaned around and followed his gaze. They'd finally reached the northlands.

The sky held a swath of silver-grey, remnants of the sand storm that had cleared up only an hour before. A persistent chill refused to leave Talis as he rode. He'd tried to cast Fire Mage to warm himself up, but he was unable to concentrate. He was tired and windswept and missed the warmth of his home. And he missed his family. From the downward glances of the others, they were exhausted too.

He scanned the landscape and couldn't spot a good place to rest for the night. A part of him wanted to ride ahead and confer with Rikar about their options, but his arms and face were cold and unresponsive. They had to find a place to rest ahead. Otherwise, with the temperature dropping quickly, and without food for sustenance, he knew they've likely freeze to death.

They rode to the top of a hill and scanned the other side. Talis released a small shout of joy as he spotted a pack of caribou, their proud horns bent down as they grazed on whatever bits of grass and lichen they could find. Hunger surged in him. The beautiful creatures raised their heads and stared at them. White mist billowed from their nostrils as they chewed, studying the approaching riders.

Talis came alongside Rikar and Nikulo's horse as they drooled at the beasts. "I think we've found our dinner," Nikulo whispered.

Mara withdrew her bow and nocked an arrow. "First to strike the prey gets the first bite. Let's go!"

Talis and Mara sped off after the caribou, and Rikar and Nikulo flanked around. The pack bolted off, but a young buck, confused at the two horses coming at him from different directions turned to face Talis and Mara, and pawed at the ground. A moment too late he charged off after the pack, but Mara's arrow caught him in the ribs, and a second shot hit his right flank. Stumbling, the buck kicked, huffing and grunting, and big white exhalations floated off in the cold air as he fell.

Rikar leapt off his horse, and brought his sword down to end the poor creature's pain. They would feed well tonight and probably for the next few days. They hefted the young buck onto a horse, and Rikar scanned around as if looking for a place to setup camp.

Talis dismounted and gazed at the thickening sky: big clumps of snow drifted slowly to the ground. This was the first time he'd seen snowflakes this big. His horse neighed and stomped her hooves as he stared over the vast expanse. A wide, frothy river flowed down from the north and curved east. On either side of the river were rocky clearings and thick, towering pines. Beyond, a mist settled over the river and the forest, obliterating the view of the lower mountains. However snow-capped peaks poked out halfway up in the sky, like sentinels keeping watch over their domain.

"This must be the Turyan River. And beyond, the Elbegurian Forest," Talis said, his voice low and tense. "Master Holoron said these were dangerous lands...."

"But it looks so beautiful," Mara said, sliding her arm through his. Blade-edged peaks and granite faces ten thousand feet tall. Wind whipped near the peaks and blew snow in enormous cotton swaths. One peak held a massive glacier…a thick cap of ice and snow. Talis stood transfixed, and glanced down at the forests. He'd never seen such gigantic trees. Closer to the river, the pines were hundreds of feet tall. But further up, titanic trees towered over the land, with the top halves of the trees bursting above the fog. A cold, dark power filled the land, and Talis could feel it tingle under his skin. He stared at the lower forest as if eyes were everywhere, watching them.

"Let's camp over there, on the left side of the river, along the tree line," Rikar said. "We'll make a fine roast tonight."

Mara and Talis followed Nikulo and Rikar's horse as they rode down the hillside towards the river. The wind was fierce now, and the snow dumped down in droves. Twilight settled as they made their way through the rocky clearing and reached the forest's edge.

Talis slid off his horse and staggered, as his legs tried to recover from the long ride. A gnaw in his stomach reminded him that he hadn't eaten in almost two days.

Rikar and Talis removed the packs while Mara and Nikulo searched around for wood. Soon they'd gathered enough and Rikar released a fiery stream into the wood, and big puffs of smoke shot into the sky. They built a roasting spit and Rikar skinned the buck. Talis sat, watching Nikulo's masterful roasting skills, and listened to the fat sizzle, inhaling the sweet smell.

Once the roast was ready, Talis reminded Nikulo to give the first slice to Mara. Her radiant eyes accepted the food and she ate it slowly, as if mindful of her stomach's emptiness. Talis ate a helping, then ate some more until his belly felt like it would explode. Food had never tasted so good. After the meal, color returned to Mara's pretty face and she sat next to him, curled up, and lay her head on his lap. He thought he heard her purring with content as she fell asleep.

The next day Talis woke to find Mara's arms entangled around his waist. It wasn't an unpleasant feeling to have her so close, her small figure warming him through the cold night. He brushed aside a lock of hair from her face and found her lips moving as she enjoyed food in a dream. She was beautiful, he realized. Perhaps even more so to Talis now that he found comfort in having her companionship along their journey to that island far away. He couldn't bear the thought of being away from her.

Rikar chuckled deviously, and Talis spun around to catch his jeering eyes. He wagged his head from side-to-side as if he thought Talis hopelessly in love. Talis resisted a harsh retort, not wanting to wake Mara from her sleep. Rikar seemed to notice his concern for Mara, so he opened his mouth and shouted an imitation of a crow's call.

Talis flinched as he felt Mara seize his arms.

"What was that?" she said, her voice groggy and tired.

"You bastard," Talis said to Rikar, and gave him the hand salute inviting him to go straight to hell.

"Time to wake up and go." Rikar pushed himself up and collected his things. "Go while the day is still young."

Nikulo groaned and rolled over to stare bleary-eyed at Rikar. "Did you have to wake me up with your ridiculous imitation of a dying crow? Stick to magic and sword play, your animal calls sound more like the agonizing mating calls of ducks."

Mara laughed and glanced with gleeful eyes at Nikulo's now rumbling form. "Stop making me laugh...gods, I have to pee." She got up and ran over to the trees and disappeared behind a boulder.

By the time she returned Talis, Rikar, and Nikulo had finished packing their horses. Rikar brought out a dagger and was carving up the remains of the roast. He brought out a leather skin and wrapped and bound the meat. They mounted their horses and trotted off towards the water.

After trekking along the river for several hours, they found a trail leading north. Talis studied the Surineda Map and realized they were heading towards the village of Blansko. Half a day's journey in they found the trail obliterated by an enormous rockslide that had felled giant soldier pines, creating an unsurpassable mess. Rikar suggested they loop around to the east and follow the river north. But before they reached the river, tall boulders hundreds of feet high stopped their way.

The only way to go was through the dark, pine forest. The branches pressed down at many places so low they had to dismount their horses and lead them through. They followed Rikar as he trudged through the forest, slowing as the woods enveloped them. There was something soothing about the fragrant air infused with pine and mountain herbs, and the calm from being shield by the wind. Almost too calm.

Talis inhaled a gulp of air and walked on after Rikar. A commotion above moved the limbs against each other. The eerie croaking and groaning of wood against wood. The sound unnerved Talis, but Mara smiled at him with kind eyes, and they kept on.

"Over there," he said, pointing with his chin. They kept ahead towards a patch of twilight beyond the forest. After reaching a clearing filled with logs and boulders, he saw that the way continued into an even deeper forest.

He sighed. "Still more to go."

After a long hike through a dense, suffocating part of the forest, lit torches now in hand, they found an old tree lying on the ground, with termites devouring the wood. Too tired to go on, they decided to rest here for the night.

Talis knocked branches off the tree and grinned as he kicked another branch. It cracked and shattered in several pieces. He made a game where he was snapping the necks off Jiserian necromancers. It helped. Mara picked up a branch and swirled it around, giggling.

"This place is creepy." She poked Talis.

"Are you kidding? I'm so glad we're out of the desert." Talis spun around, trying to trip Mara. She jumped, and darted out of the way.

"Would you two stop messing around?" Rikar sighed. "Just get some wood for a fire."

Mara stuck out her tongue at Rikar, and punched at Nikulo's big belly. He blocked and danced left.

Readying another jab to the ribs, Mara stopped and looked up.

"What's wrong?" Talis said, following her gaze.

"Not sure. I just had a weird feeling."

Then he caught an awful smell. A mixture of wet, decaying leaves and fermented wheat. His shoulders stiffened.

"Light a fire so we can see better," she said. The air had turned quiet and lifeless, and he wanted exactly the same thing as she. There was something here in the forest—with them—watching them.

"Let's gather some branches," he said, his voice urgent. Mara nodded and they got to work.

Rikar glanced around and raised his torch. "Are you guys just trying to freak me out?"

"No," Talis said, shrugging. "It's just strange here."

"All right—" Rikar froze in his tracks as Mara screamed.

Talis whipped around and spotted her cringing on the ground, mouth gaping, horrified eyes staring up.

13

Assault in the Forest

Up high in the branches Talis could see hundreds of wriggling spiders. Four feet across and covered in a fine, hairy-sheen, they drooled something black and wet a glob of which sizzled on the leaves nearby. Their yellow beady eyes shone, staring hungrily at them as they descended on scores of thin, silvery cords. Talis rushed over to protect Mara. The horses whinnied and fled the forest.

Just as a spider dropped over her, Mara rolled aside and whipped out her daggers. She slashed out, slicing off legs and jumping back from spider wounds that dribbled out noxious fluids. Talis had grabbed his bow and quiver and raced to help, but his foot tripped on a root and he fell face first in the dirt, his bow flying out of his hands.

Two spiders headed towards him and more charged at Rikar and Nikulo. They had to get out of here. There were too many spiders to fight. Three of them lurched at Mara and she dove away and slashed

again with her daggers. Talis picked up his bow and
shot one in the back, sending a green spray through
the air. The others zig-zagged over the forest floor as
they chased Mara. Rikar ran after her but got in the
way of Talis's line of sight.

"Move!" Talis shouted, and darted after them.

Mara's foot landed in a hole and she fell and rolled
hard, her daggers skidding across the ground. She
glanced back as the spiders hovered over her, then
scrambled to find her weapons. Rikar zapped a spider
with a lightning bolt, generating a burned insect smell.
Another spider turned, coiled up and prepared to
strike Rikar. Talis launched another arrow, missed the
arachnoid, then shot another, sending the creature
spinning in a green, twirling mess. It splat on a tree
and its juices started eating away at the bark. What
kind of poison was that? Talis realized that the spider's
bodies were filled with acid.

"Don't waste your magic," Nikulo shouted, running up to Rikar. "There are too many of them."

"Behind you," Mara yelled.

Turning, Talis spotted one mid-flight in its jump at them. Rikar quickly summoned a silvery sword and sliced the spider in half. More charged. He flinched, stabbing and cutting the fat beasts until a pile of green spider parts and goo lay at his feet.

"Don't touch it…it's *acid!*" Talis shouted, pulling Rikar's arm.

Mara backed into a corner, surrounded by spiders. She slashed stubbornly and they snapped forward and flinched back. Every time he scanned around, more kept coming. He shot the two creatures surrounding Mara, but others charged her. Talis felt a furry leg brush his hair. He fell, aiming up, and sank an arrow into another's fat underside. He rolled away as it splattered onto the ground.

Talis grunted. He was out of arrows and there were far too many of them. He grabbed a thick stick and glanced around. Yellow eyes danced in the dark. Mara went to slice a leg off, but another curled up and hurled a sticky glob of venom over her face.

She froze and fell over. Talis felt his heart sink down to his stomach.

He charged at the spider, yelling and kicking it away from her. He brought the stick down hard against its neck and enjoyed the satisfying crunch the blow made as the creature was killed.

Nikulo huffed up to them and stared at Mara. "What happened?"

"She's poisoned," Talis said, and slammed a fist on his leg.

"We've got to get out of here," Nikulo said. Sweat poured down the sides of his head, and his eyes shone. A huge spider followed him, as if tamed and obeying his command. His hands were over his temples as he stared at the creature. It scampered over the ground and grappled two more spiders charging at them.

The creatures were everywhere. Hundreds of yellow, gleaming eyes locked on them.

"Which way do we go?" Nikulo said, and twirled around.

Rikar was feverish, exhausted from his use of magic. He summoned a curved blade, shimmering five feet across, and slashed as fast as he could. But he was tiring and in danger of being consumed by the power of magic raging through him.

"Be careful," Nikulo yelled, whirling around to face his friend. Rikar was drenched in sweat and his eyes were locked, unfocused.

Talis knew he had to act, so he began breathing loudly, a hissing breath, the kind used to create Fire Magic. In a trance, the forest had to Talis's eyes turned blood-red. Nikulo reached out to stop him, then jerked his hand back in pain.

"Get down!" Talis shouted, and Rikar and Nikulo dropped. Through the haze of his view, Talis could see the spiders closing in on them from all sides.

An intense heat ignited from his palms and exploded out in all directions, a circular wave of fire ripping through the forest. Spiders burst into flames and curled up, and the trees shuddered under the sudden inferno. The air smelled of smoky pine and burnt hair and roasted chicken. Rikar and Nikulo stood and glanced around, shocked that the forest was aflame. They were surrounded by a circle of angry flames and the fire roared out of control, dashing up the trees.

Talis stared at what he'd done. How did he cast the spell without killing himself? He felt very weak from the exertion, but his senses burned, vivid and alive.

"That was amazing!" Rikar said, his eyes surprised. "How did you cast that spell?"

"I…I'm not sure how I cast it…" Talis glanced around, concerned that the flames were stalking towards them. "But we're going to die if we don't get out of here soon."

"Help me carry Mara." Nikulo bent down and they lifted Mara and hobbled in a direction with fewer flames. Rikar seized his things as he lumbered behind. The fire ring extended out a hundred feet, and as they skirted around the fire, Talis glanced over his shoulder. *I did it, I really did it right*, he thought, and felt a wave of confidence wash over him.

As they left the burning forest, Talis couldn't help but notice Rikar and Nikulo glancing at him, their faces beaming awe and jealously. Finally they reached a bed of soft pine needles, and they lay Mara down.

Talis clenched Mara's hand and searched for signs of life, but her body was rigid but still warm.

"She's still breathing, but her body is all clenched up by the poison."

Nikulo interrupted him. "Rikar, can you hold Mara? I'll need to give her a potion. The spider's venom…locked the flow of electrical energy. If I can only release the poison's hold." He placed both hands on Mara's jawbones and his hands shook with intensity, waves of healing light flowing out. When the light built up inside her body, Mara's face softened and the tension in her muscles melted away.

Then Nikulo took off his backpack and withdrew a sack containing several crystal vials. He noticed a glob of poison sizzling away at her jacket, and he took a knife and scooped it up, placing it inside one of the vials. Talis glimpsed a delighted smile cross Nikulo's face as if he'd just discovered something incredible.

"One more herbal remedy, and I think that will do it…" Nikulo rummaged through another bag from his pack while Rikar assembled wood and lit a warm, crackling fire. Nikulo pulled out a potion, and inspected it with satisfaction. He opened Mara's mouth and poured the liquid down her throat. Her eyes fluttered and color slowly returned to her cheeks.

Mara squinted and glanced around suspiciously.

"Why is everyone staring at me?" She tried to get up but Talis held her back.

"Rest—give yourself some time to recover."

Talis told her the story of what had happened after she was poisoned and Nikulo interrupted to tell the part about Talis casting magic. Mara settled back, her face flushed from the fire, and with proud, beaming eyes smiled at Talis. She reached out to hold his hand and soon she drifted off to sleep.

He felt a wave of homesickness strike his heart as he gazed at Mara's face. She could have died out here in this cold and unforgiving land, and Talis knew he could never forgive himself if that had ever happened. Yet Naru might already be in more danger than here. Perhaps another attack had killed more people… The Elders of Naru were counting on them to help their city. Talis told himself he was right to insist on continuing on their expedition. Every day counted.

"We've lost our horses and whatever we had in our saddlebags." Rikar glanced at the dark forest.

Talis swung his backpack around. "Let's see what we have… I kept a good bit of gold and silver coin inside. We can resupply and maybe buy horses up ahead at the inn."

"What do you think we'll find out there on that island?" Nikulo said, his eyes tired and red.

Talis shrugged, and stared into the fire. "It must be worth it…worth all the risk. You weren't there to see Master Baribariso rise from the grave and transform into an immortal. When he pulled the Surineda Map from a mist, I knew this was a true gift from the gods."

"There are many gods and many masters," Rikar said, his face dark and gaunt. "But I do not doubt there is something powerful and special out there on that island…." Talis pictured prostrated Rikar worshiping Zagros, Lord of the Underworld, and wondered how many more dark gods and masters Rikar followed.

"Something that could help in our struggle against the Jiserians?" Nikulo warmed his hands on the fire.

They watched the fire for what seemed like an ageless moment, and the heat felt good sinking into Talis's cold hands. After he'd cast the spell against the spiders it seemed like all the warmth had left his body, and the chill of the northlands had possessed him.

A sputter of sparks shook them out of their reverie, and Talis looked at Rikar, recognizing a wave of pain and darkness flash across his face. Rikar turned away, flushed with discomfort, and Talis wished he knew what dark thoughts passed through his mind….

The next morning Mara pranced around bright and cheerful as if fully recovered. They set out early and hiked along the Turyan River, snaking left and right and up through massive, granite boulders. After an hour or so they arrived at a series of waterfalls. The first one was about fifteen feet high and stretched across the length of the river. Beyond, more waterfalls fell over jagged cliffs and tunneled through the pine forest.

Talis stopped and inhaled the crisp mountain air, peering up at the falls. "How do we get around—"

"I found a path up ahead…there on the left." Rikar pointed and started towards the trail.

Mist shimmered off the rocks as they climbed up around the falls and Mara stretched out her tongue and enjoyed the cool spray. The boulders glistened under the sun's rays and the air seemed charged with power. The mountains were more amazing than Talis had ever dreamed. All his life he'd lived in an oasis surrounded by desert. He loved Naru, but the forest and the mountains of the northlands made him feel like a mouse among giants.

Rikar led them up the path as it curved, climbing higher through the boulders. At this height, Talis could see the river disappear and merge into the distant desert. He was leaving the desert and Naru behind. There was no going back. He'd left his family and he might not ever return home.

After the sun plunged below the mountains, they reached a field filled with apple trees. Farther up, they passed a barn and heard rapids churning down the river. An inn lay ahead with billowing smoke rising from a chimney. Stone walls and a slate roof so heavy it seemed as if the rafters would crumble under the weight. Wooden shutters covered the windows and a glow of orange light shone through. Talis tensed as a group of travelers milled out front, their clothes tattered, faces dirty and gaunt, eyes hopeless and suspicious.

They stared, watching them approach.

14

The Inn at Blansko

Talis strode towards the inn, stripping off his pack and he straightened his back as he neared the front steps. He was so exhausted and cold he could barely walk straight. All he thought of was food and fire at the hearth and sleep. The front door opened with a creak as he let Mara enter first, then he stepped into the warm glow. The air smelled like the roasts back home at the fall festival, of pork and smoke and sweet pies. He inhaled and found himself drooling.

The great room was lined with cedar planks and pine beams spanned almost forty feet across. The once noisy room grew quiet as they entered and all eyes turned and stared with suspicion. The barkeep, a short stocky man wearing a bloodied apron, scanned the newcomers as he ran his stubby fingers through his beard.

His expression darkened. "What do you want?"

Talis strolled forward and handed the man a silver coin. "Food...and drink, for me and my friends."

The barkeep inspected the coin. "From Naru—long ways from home, aren't you?"

"If you care to show us to a table." Talis tapped his finger on the worn, wooden bar-top.

The barkeep grunted, as if annoyed by his comment, then motioned Talis towards an empty table.

The tension melted and the room went back to talking, eating, and drinking. Two girls, of a similar age to Talis, sat together on a wooden bench next to the fire. They wore white silk dresses with lavender flowers embroidered along the bottom trim. One girl was taller and had vibrant silver hair and a mousy face. The other girl had flaming red hair and long, dangling earrings. Her cherubic face was painted white and chalky, cheeks rouged, a seven-pronged star drawn on her forehead.

Could she be a mystic? Legend had it that they were trained in the arts starting at age three: to read faces, minds, tea leaves, the wind, animal bones, and even read the future. Their powers were legendary, and it was said that royal houses all over the world valued them at court for their divination skills.

Turning their heads, they giggled as Talis sauntered towards the fireplace, blushing when they caught his gaze. The girl with the star seemed to know some secret about him that she was unwilling to share. Mara darted past and plopped herself onto a bench opposite the girls. He warmed his hands then sat next to Mara, yawning sloppily.

"I'm hungry and sleepy at the same time." He glanced at the girl with the star, her grey-sapphire eyes danced as he looked at her. She whispered into the silver-haired girl's ear and laughed, tossing her head back, sending her long hair flying about.

The silver-haired girl blurted out, "Is she your girlfriend?"

The other girl paused a moment, leaned forward, and gazed into his eyes. Talis couldn't break from her stare, and he could feel Mara seething next to him.

"Not yet..." the girl with the star said mysteriously. She laughed freely. "He doesn't know a thing. Boys...." Mara blushed as he glanced at her, and Talis wondered if what the mystic said could be true.

Heavy footsteps sounded as Rikar and Nikulo sauntered over to the fire and eyed the girls with unconcealed attraction.

"I've never seen a girl with silver hair." Rikar grinned wolfishly at her.

She huffed, rolling her eyes. "Maybe if you took a bath more often girls could actually stand being around you."

Talis chuckled, then stopped, realizing he probably smelled just as bad.

"You're travelers…like us? From the west perhaps?" Nikulo said.

"We're just passing through," said the girl with the star, and glanced shyly at Talis. "This is my sister Nuella." Her eyes locked sweetly with Talis for a moment, and she said, "And I'm Lenora."

Rikar bowed, trying to act like a perfect nobleman, but came off like he was arrogant and pretentious. He introduced everyone, staring way too much at Nuella in the process. She suppressed a glare each time he looked at her. Rikar was too stupid to even realize it.

Lenora bowed awkwardly, and sniffed suspiciously. "You're runaways, like us."

"We're hardly like you," Mara said, her tone sharp and dismissive. Talis chuckled as Mara stared contemptuously at them.

"Now, now, no fighting." Nikulo tilted his head at Lenora and smiled. "But we're no runaways, we're on a quest of sorts."

Lenora ignored Mara, and lowered her voice as she leaned forward. "Our city was destroyed by the Jiserians. Burned to the ground. Only a few of us escaped with our lives."

"Father says we're lucky." Nuella frowned as if unconvinced. "I miss my mother and our home. I miss the parties and the dances and the knights in silver and gold."

Talis stared at the fire, knowing the same fate could happen to Naru. He glanced up at Lenora. "You're a mystic?"

Lenora flushed. "I was trained as one…not seasoned, not tested by Sisters yet. Too late for all that."

"Never too late." Nuella ran a finger along her sister's arm. "You remember what Sister Eayla said…about the wind, the wind speaking to you."

"I haven't heard a thing from the wind yet…I just hear mother's screams, that's all I hear inside." Lenora touched the side of her head, and looked at her hand as if wondering what it was doing.

"After crossing the desert and these barbaric woods, I'm in dire need of a drink." Nikulo sighed. "Ale anyone? Cider? Red wine?"

"Father doesn't let us drink… He says we're too young."

"Nonsense," Nikulo said, devilish twist on his mouth. "In times such as these, ale does the soul good."

"Well I suppose… If you insist." Lenora grinned as if she were willing to hide anything from her father.

Nikulo trotted towards the tavern owner, and returned with several mugs, handing them to the girls first. They glanced around the room nervously and peered inside.

"I tried the ale… You wouldn't like it." Nikulo hiccupped. "I tried the wine too—dreadful. You wouldn't like that either. Hard cider seemed like the best option. Harvest time of the year, after all." He nodded his head knowingly at Nuella and lifted his mug in a toast. "To youth and beauty… May you always refuse to die."

Lenora took a sip, and whispered, "Does your quest have anything to do with the Jiserians?"

Talis edged closer to Lenora. "We share a common foe. Just last week, our city, Naru, was attacked by Jiserian sorcerers. But they haven't defeated us yet…at least I hope not."

"Do you have any idea how powerful the Jiserians are?" Rikar said, and squinted at Talis. "Without the most powerful of magic, we'll be useless against them. You haven't got a clue what is needed." He drank the cider, and wiped the sides of his mouth.

"But we can stop them." Mara glared at Rikar. "That's why we're on our quest. To turn things in our favor."

Lenora looked doubtful. "Father is leading us to Khael. He says that Khael and the lands to the north are free from the Jiserian's grasp—"

"Father said they are allied yet protected," Nuella interrupted, her voice filled with uncertainty. According to Master Holoron, the city of Khael was an outlaw city, filled with pirates and brigands. If Khael was allied with the Jiserians, Talis knew they probably wouldn't be welcome. But they needed to go through Khael to find ship's passage to the island.

A man's deep voice shouted, and Talis jerked his head around to see a big man with sagging jowls and darting eyes stomping over towards them. He glowered at Talis and Rikar and seized the mugs from the girls' hands. "What are you doing? You should know better by now. Why are you talking to *these* people? And why are you drinking this!" He fixed his eyes on Talis and looked him up and down, and huffed, the smell of garlic and liver wafting from his mouth.

"I think you misunderstood, *Father*," Lenora said, standing firm. "These travelers are from Naru, recently attacked by the Jiserians—"

"Naru? You can't seriously be from Naru. But why would the Jiserians dare attack your city?"

The man relaxed his shoulders, and studied Talis more closely. Fears assuaged, he sat next to his daughter, the bench groaning under his weight. He glanced back and forth between Talis and Rikar, wringing his hands as if they were wet.

"Don't pay any mind to my gruffness... Besides, who can trust strangers?" He smiled, as if trying to assure them that his suspicion was natural. "Tell me, has Naru fallen to those foul Jiserians?"

"Nay." Rikar put a whetstone to his dagger. "We repelled their aerial invasion. Unlike, it sounds, your village...."

"Not a village lad, a great city, Bechamel Downs, laid to waste by hoards of Jiserian mongrels. Strange beasts, made of mud and sticks and twisted vines. They sieged our city for weeks, as if toying with us. Those bastards sent us petitions for our surrender each night at dusk. But our foolish leaders refused each time—"

"I've never heard of your city." Rikar twisted up his face. "Well it doesn't surprise me, honestly, your leaders probably sold you out in exchange for titles in the new Jiserian Empire...people do that, you know. They did it at Onair and countless other cities along the western coast."

"Who are you, boy?" Lenora's father said. "You talk as if you're a king—"

"Perhaps one day... Mother says that's a possibility." Rikar looked up at the beams, eyes blinking rapidly.

"The Lei Family line is in waiting for the throne," Mara said, her voice terse.

"They'll be waiting a long time if they're dead. Enough of this talk." Rikar stared at Lenora's father. "Our party is in shambles...ruined by an attack from Jiserian necromancers in the desert. Your daughter here tells us you're traveling to Khael. Yes? Good, we are also traveling to the coast... Shall we bind together, safety in numbers and all that?"

"I don't see why not." Lenora's father shook his fat jowls left and right. "Yes, it's decided. Travel with us to Khael, join me and my daughters, and our two servants. Together we'll be nine."

"We'll need to talk it over...as a group." Mara glanced at Talis.

"All this talk is making me hungry." Nikulo jutted his chin at their table. The barkeep had just set down a huge bowl of stew filled with pork and cabbage and potatoes, and roasted bread, topped with what looked like garlic and butter. It smelled better than it looked.

"If I didn't have the gift of sight," Lenora said, "I wouldn't say our paths are intertwined. Because they are. Somehow the way ahead is made clearer after meeting you...."

The way she spoke made Talis feel as if fate had spoken. If he resisted, the gods would be angered. For a brief moment, when she had voiced the words, it was as if time stilled and her eyes were illuminated with some strange fire. He couldn't resist staring at her even if he tried.

Mara elbowed him in the ribs. "Snap out of it." She yanked his arm and led him to the table.

Talis was about to grumble, then he thought the better of it. When Mara was determined like that it was impossible to say a thing. He filled his bowl and ate, thinking about Lenora. She might be a mystic, but from Mara's expression of contempt, Lenora was a witch.

15

The Edge of the Storm

When Rikar and Nikulo and Talis all agreed to travel with Lenora and her family, Mara was furious. She promised them no good would come from traveling with those strangers. But Talis couldn't help notice the edge of jealousy in her voice. After all, Lenora was beautiful and from an exotic kingdom, and he was curious to discover the secrets of the mystic school of magic.

Rikar and Talis had found enough gold in their purses to buy four horses, the last of which was a small, fat horse that seemed perfectly suited for Nikulo (despite his protests). Talis glanced up as a stable boy finished placing a saddle and bags onto his speckled grey horse. He handed a small silver coin to the boy, and grinned as the boy's eyes went wide staring at the coin.

A stiff wind sent the cypress trees swaying above. The horses whinnied, spurred by the unsettled air. Talis thought of Naru, and vowed he'd never forgive himself if anything happened to his family. They had to stay focused and remain steadfast in their goal of quickly reaching the island.

As he mounted his horse, he gazed east and found his heart filling with a strange sense of foreboding. What was out there waiting for them? His thoughts were interrupted as Mara rode up alongside.

"I still don't think this is a good idea." Her white horse circled around, as if anxious to begin the ride.

"We can always go off on our own if it doesn't work out with them."

She came in close, and whispered, "Have you seen those *servants* Lenora's father was talking about? More like an evil-looking sorceress and a grim reaper with a scimitar... We carry the most valuable relic in the world, how can you trust them? When it was just innocent-looking Nuella, that witch Lenora, and her fat father, it seemed harmless."

Talis chuckled, not imagining Mara could ever be so jealous. "She's not nearly as pretty as you."

Mara blushed, and looked stunned and elated for a moment. She opened her mouth to retort when Rikar and Nikulo rode up, followed by Lenora and her sister. Nikulo's horse seemed to strain under the weight.

"And what joker thought it was funny to give me this horse?"

"Why you're perfectly matched." Mara tried to stifle a snicker.

Lenora's father trotted up in a big black mare, flanked by the sorceress and the blademaster. "Enough talk, we need to ride hard to reach the mountain pass by nightfall."

The sorceress stared at Talis as if searching for clues. He felt a heat prickle under his skin, recognizing her use of magic. He knew he had to stay guarded against her magical senses.

They left the village and took a spindly trail to a bridge suspended between two huge boulders. The river flowed hundreds of feet below. The horse's hooves clapped against the wood as they trotted ahead. Talis made the mistake of peering down at the steep drop and felt his head spin from the vertigo. The river raged and frothed below him.

In the warming of late afternoon, the sky cleared and Talis lifted his eyes and his mouth fell open. Sheer granite cliffs towered over them, to the left and to the right, rising to the zenith. The glow of the sun reflected off the cliffs, creating a wash of brilliant light. Sentinel pines a thousand feet tall stood guard at the entrance of a pass that knifed through the mountains. But the mountains dwarfed those pines, rising seven or eight times higher. How were such mountains formed, he wondered?

The next morning they trekked inside the dark pass, torches in hand to guide them through the darkness, and they curved up and around through the pass until they broke out of the narrow corridor and reached twilight on the other side. They'd climbed several thousand feet and the air was now cold and dry. Swept before them were mountain lakes and sheer, jutting granite spires dotting the carpet of spruce and redwood and cedar. Talis loved the mountains and the invigorating, fragrant smell of pine, with the wind racing through rocks and branches. The shade of trees provided sanctuary from the unyielding sun, and when thirsty, the taste of sweet water from mountain springs wet their mouths from the dryness in the air.

After two days of riding through the forests, the once fair horizon turned dark and cloudy and the air chilled as night approached. The horses whinnied nervously and caused Talis to feel a strange sense of maliciousness in the swirling skies.

The blademaster stiffened and gazed at the sky. "Storm's brewing."

Talis studied the thick grey and black clouds churning high above. Fierce sudden winds shook the treetops and the leaves and needles danced with each gust. The invigorating air of storm and pine and cedar rushed into his lungs. It was as if nature were a crouched mountain lion, ready to pounce on its next victim. A drop of rain splashed into his eye and another landed on his chin. With a storm as fierce as this seemed, they'd need to seek shelter for the night.

Soon rain pelted his face and hair, and he grimaced and pulled his hood over his head. The trees grew animated with the force of wind, rising and clawing at the clouds like specters. Large sheets of rain painted the grey sky in a wet, willowy wash. For a time he felt warm and protected in his wool cloak, but very soon under the dumping rain he was drenched.

The blademaster tried his best to keep the party moving in a straight line, despite the wind lashing their horses around in a frenzy. Waves of leaves and rain made it impossible to see. Talis could feel the agitation of his horse under the erratic wind—her nostrils flared and she shook her head in contempt. Each moment a struggle, and each minute darker, he wished he were back in the warm comfort of the inn. The suffocating air from the low clouds caused a constriction in his chest, making each breath more difficult than the last.

A sudden vast movement in the sky whipped the wind stronger, and the wind rushed through the trees and howled in fury. Limbs cracked, branches flew and smashed against tree trunks. With the wind came an outpouring of torrential rain—the kind that reaches inside you and claws and digs and squirms, until you want to scream.

Talis glanced around, then kicked his horse and sped up to the blademaster. "We need shelter. I can barely stay on my horse."

"Where?" the blademaster yelled, his strained eyes searching.

Talis blinked, wiped his eyes, and inspected the forest. Far off in the darkness, he spotted a faint flicker of light. The storm made it nearly impossible to see, but the light was there again, stronger now. Maybe it was a village? He stopped and turned his horse. He pointed at the light and the others squinted in desperation.

The blademaster nodded and led them on towards the light. One light expanded into many lights dancing through the trees. Talis relaxed when he realized that he was right, they'd found a village. Huts glowed and glimmered from fires inside. Smoke wafted out. He rode around to the middle of a circle of huts and jumped at the sight of an old man sitting under a canopy attached to a hut. A serene smile crossed the man's face as he stared at the newcomers. He wore tattered animal skins, as if from a hunt done years ago.

The blademaster wielded his sword out of instinct, but softened as the man lifted his hands and bowed in supplication.

"Take shelter from the elements, friends. I'm known as Barnabus, leader of our humble village." He motioned them inside. "Be our guests and warm yourselves by our fires."

Talis glanced around and a chill shimmied up his scalp. Other old women and men poked their heads out of the huts, their eyes held a tired, hungry look, as if receiving the first, youthful visitors in years.

Sliding off his horse, the blademaster sheathed his sword as scanned the huts with wary eyes. The wind gusted as he took refuge under the canopy of the village leader. The sorceress followed the soldier, and the smell of roasted meat entered Talis's nostrils as the woman went inside the hut. After a moment, their companion poked his head out and waved at the others. Talis licked his lips, and imagined the taste of the roast.

Barnabus led Talis and Mara past several sloping huts. Aged men and women stared at them as they passed, and in those stares Talis saw the kind of sadness that lingers in the mind for many years. Their faces were filled with harsh wrinkles and their backs were hunched over like wretches. Barnabus opened a flap to a round hut and led them inside.

"Our village is humble and our huts small," he said. "But you're welcome to stay until the storm clears."

By a low fire in the center of the room, an old woman stirred an iron pot filled with stew. She wore a white lace apron over a frumpy black robe. She smiled with soft, caring eyes as they entered. Her long silvery hair was tied up in an elaborately twisted bun. She reminded Talis of his grandmother—always cooking stew on cold, wintry days.

He bowed to her, feeling gratitude flood his heart. "Thank you for your hospitality."

As he pulled off his drenched cloak and laid it on a bench near the fire, he caught her motherly glance at his wet clothes. He realized he was soaked to the bone. Shivering, he hovered around the flames, feeling life return to his hands. He sighed as the warmth seeped into his body. Now if he could just sleep—no, he was hungry. He couldn't decide what to do first.

The old crone coughed slightly. "Welcome home, my son. What's kept you away these long years? You've made a mother's heart grow sad, longing for her son." She touched his shoulder and a million lines of electricity shot through his body. His eyes went wide, but he brushed off the feeling, refusing it real. He tried to imagine what it must be like for this poor old woman to be abandoned by her son.

"Let's get you out of these wet clothes." She ambled over to a wooden chest in the corner and it creaked as she opened the lid. She peered inside and after chewing her lip for a while pulled out a green shirt and brown cotton pants. He eyed her cautiously as he accepted the gift.

"Would your lady friend be needing some clothes to change into as well?"

Mara nodded and rubbed her arms, looking hesitantly at Talis. It was far too quiet. After they'd entered, it seemed the storm had calmed down to nothing. Even the wind ceased. But Talis was glad for the fire, for it melted away his cold and fatigue. He was so exhausted that he couldn't think. Besides, he told himself, the woman was old and decrepit. Many old people in Naru had lost a bit of their minds.

The woman tottered back to the chest and pulled out a white gown. She lifted the gown, glanced at Mara, then smiled and waddled over to her. "These clothes should fit you. My daughter wore them before the wind took her away." Her eyes glistened and her face held the look of a mother betrayed by her children. Talis imagined his sister, Lia—how could she ever leave mother? They were inseparable.

Mara ran her fingers over the silky gown, then noticed Talis watching her. She held it over her chest, blushed, and searched the room for a place to change. She went behind the bed and Talis turned to let her dress.

"Much better." She returned to the fire, face beaming at him in her pretty gown, and she let the heat from the fire sink into her hands.

Talis removed his vest and shirt, and glanced up, noticing her curious eyes. She looked down shyly. He grabbed the fresh clothes and strode over to the corner and found a quilt. He lifted it over his body and she giggled at him as he tried to change holding the quilt. He stumbled and dropped it several times, revealing his nakedness, and she broke into a fit of embarrassed chuckles when he returned to the fire.

The old woman carried their wet clothes and hung them on a cord. She sat, returning to stirring the stew. The smell of wild game and onions wafted through the air, making his stomach gurgle in anticipation.

Talis collapsed onto a bearskin, too exhausted even to ask for food. His skin flushed as he faced the fire, and found his eyes drooping from the warm glow.

"So comfortable." He yawned, wanting nothing other than to close his eyes and sleep.

Mara slipped in beside him, lying behind with her arm wrapped over his chest. The heat from the fire and her hand on his chest slowly drained him of the desire to keep his eyes open. He blinked and nodded off, still feeling the pouring rain and the wind hammering his neck. In his mind, the trees still swayed back and forth, with sheets of rain pelting his face.

The light in the hut dimmed. The room was quiet save the soft clacking of the wooden ladle against the iron pot. Mara pressed closer, so close he felt her chest snug against his back, and soon he found himself drifting off. Faintly, as if off in a dream world, he thought he heard the sound of drums.

16

Ashtera Summons the Darkness

Shadows stretched long and thin and wound around the corner to the sleepy hut. Talis bolted awake in a fright. A horrendous scream, tormented and deep, echoed through the huts. The saddest sound, worse than a mourner's party on dreary winter's day. Who had made that cry?

Drums outside hammered out a tight rhythm of wild, beautiful frenzy.

"Wake up," he told Mara. He smelled a horrible stench and wondered where it came from. He glanced over at Mara and realized she hadn't heard a word he'd said. She was snoring. His nose pointed towards the iron pot as the source of the stench. He scrambled over and peered inside, then recoiled in terror. *What in the name of the gods?* A man's hairless head floated in the vile stew. Blanched eyes stared at nothing. He could see the exposed veins and throat where the head had been sliced off. Arms and legs and bones pressed thickly together. Talis's stomach churned, as if the contents of the stew were inside of him. He covered his mouth and fought the bile pushing up his throat.

"Gods, are those—" He stopped and looked around. *Be quiet, Talis,* he told himself. A knot now clenched in his stomach and his mind raced. *What was happening outside?*

He shook Mara, but she only turned over. "There's something wrong. Get up!" he hissed.

She rubbed her eyes and squinted at him. "What's that smell?"

He pointed at the stew and she stared into the pot, and gripped her stomach and fell back.

"Listen," he whispered. There was something terribly wrong; they'd fallen into a trap.

Drums kept pounding outside and now voices joined in, chanting strange words to match the wild rhythm.

"Talis, what's going on?" Her face was white and horrified.

"We need to look outside... But we must remain quiet and unnoticed." Stalking under the canopy, he peeked around the corner. A fever flushed through his body at what he saw. Lenora, Nuella, Rikar, and Nikulo danced around a fire filled with a ghostly green light. Bones were crumpled up inside. Talis realized that Lenora's father, the blademaster, and the sorceress were missing. A beautiful woman with long black hair stood in the center, cackling and shouting frenzied incantations. Her arms gestured seductively into the air. Talis gasped, and shrank back into the hut.

"They're all mesmerized," he whispered.

"We have to do something." Mara gathered her clothes, and they dressed quickly.

Did they even have a chance? If they tried to attack, it was two against many. The once old and useless looking men and women were renewed and powerful, their faces plump and rosy, hair full and without a speck of silver. Their skin radiated vitality and not a trace of their former wrinkles remained. Now they stood with a straight, confident posture and they danced and twirled like euphoric fools.

Talis remembered the battle in the desert. *Destroy the leader and the rest will fall.* "Attack the witch—the woman with the long black hair. Let's go around behind and surprise them." He wielded his sword and felt the fire slither up his arm.

He followed Mara outside and together they found a place to hide in the shadows. The dancers gyrated their bodies and surrounded the leader as she shook her hips to the beat. Lifting her hands to the stars, she cast another spell aimed at Nikulo. His body jerked off the ground, arms and legs hanging limp.

In a panic, Mara raised her bow and fired a shot at the woman. The arrow plunged into the witch's side and she screamed and spun herself around, her furious eyes finding purchase on Mara. Another arrow struck the woman in the throat. The witch released a muffled gurgling sound as she clenched her neck, eyes wide in disbelief. Her body flapped like an injured bird fluttering on the ground. Talis charged at the woman, sword arm tensed and ready to cut her down.

The drummers stopped the music and glowered at Talis's approach. One drummer pounded a raging tune and a shock wave sent Talis tumbling across the ground. He looked up to see the witch's eyes widened, as if she were witnessing death's door. Her mouth hung open in horror and she gasped for air, like a carp plucked from a pond, but her words were trapped inside. She yanked the arrow from her neck and ripped out a chunk of bloodied flesh. A gush of blood drenched her robe and her mouth released a gurgle as she flicked her wrists and twirled around in a brilliant whirl, transforming herself into the old woman from Talis and Mara's hut.

He gaped at her in stunned silence. How could she morph like that in an instant?

As the woman seized her still-bleeding neck, anger flashed across her face. She coughed out blood mixed with ash and fell to the ground, her body writhing in frenzied convulsions. The drummers turned towards her and started a peculiar rhythm, and the singers chanted in time with the drums and mimicked the movement of the witch's seizures.

The old woman's body rocketed up into the air, arms splayed in a triumphant pose, and as she feathered to the ground, her body transformed back once again to the young witch's form. She landed smoothly and stood like a queen surveying her subjects. She shouted at the moons and released a deep, rolling laugh. When she lifted her chin, she revealed an unbroken, unblemished neck.

"I am called Ashtera by the earth goddess, who is our mother and our life. Who dares challenge me?" She let out a savage cry and Talis covered his ears at the sound. Mara flew backwards from the witch's powerful spell and skidded across the ground. She cried out in pain and clenched her temples.

"Bad girl, playing naughty games with toy weapons." The witch wagged her clawed fingers at Mara.

Talis shouted to distract the woman from Mara, and he thrust his sword at the witch's chest. She tensed her fingers, as if tightening her grip around a ball. He felt an immense pressure crush his throat and he coughed and pushed back, trying to stop the force of her power. A flow of blood streamed out of his nostril. He felt a terrific pain and knew he was dying, and understood that dying was the only way to ease the pain.

He clenched his teeth and gripped harder on his sword, greater than the crushing force around his throat. Something unlocked inside his heart, as if his hands seized the power of the sword and infused his breathing with life and his will with resolve. His mind was forged with a purpose: he must save the others. He couldn't fail them.

After he struggled to heave his sword above his head, he brought it down until the hilt was pressed against his chest. He tensed his arms and allowed the fire from the sword to surge through his body. With renewed force, he pressed back *hard* at Ashtera and an invisible hand smashed her back against the ground. He leapt at her and sliced down as she lifted terrified eyes to face him. He felt the resistance from her neck bone as it met the blade. Her head twisted and fell to one side as its came partially off the trunk. The sword glowed blood-red as it struck and he stared as ripples of fire washed through her body.

The drummers and chanters stopped and gasped in horror. The singers shrieked and sounded their sorrow. But the drummers went back and stupidly beat their drums and the singers chanted with them. All too late, for Talis's second blow lopped the witch's head off completely and sent it flying like a bloody windmill. The head lay still on the ground. Her eyes moved— searching for meaning.

Filaments of green light streamed out of her head and body. The dark life force that had sustained her streamed back into the sparkling fire. A pile of ash remained where she once lay. *I feel it*, he thought, *the fire in the sword*. He growled with power, his eyes feasting on the blade.

The chanters and drummers stood in shock. Talis spun his gaze at them. He had to kill them. As he charged, the drummers reacted, beating out an angry tune. The chanter's strained voices sang a shrill, powerful song. He flung his hands to cover his ears and his sword fell, slicing into the wet soil. Under that immense pain he crashed to his knees and howled in agony.

The drummers found a new rhythm and sent the voices of demons to invade his mind. The shock of electricity seared along the left side of his body, great jolts wracking his heart. A sudden command from a demon's voice echoed in his mind: *smash your head, use that stone, do it now!* He reached out and exhaled, fighting back against the words. For all the magic that Master Viridian had taught him, why couldn't he have said anything about resisting this kind of magic? He seized the stone and pounded the ground, then glowered at the drummers. He wouldn't stop now. He could never stop until they were dead. Jumping forward, he hammered the drummer's head and crushed his skull, sending his limp body withering back to the ground.

As he landed the kill blow, the chanters found a low, growling voice, like the sound of ocean waves gurgling through pebbles. They focused on Talis and delivered their merged power at his body. He was whipped backwards into the air until he crashed through a hut. He slammed his fist against the earth and allowed his anger to build up the fire magic inside.

The drummers sped up the rhythm until it built into a stuttered frenzy. Talis glared at them through the hut's torn flap, determined to win at any cost. They moved and swayed to the song of the chanters, the light from an unholy fire filling their eyes. Dark magic flowed from each note.

He pushed himself up and conjured flames in his mind's eye. Filled with fire, it surged in with each hissing breath, until his lungs were enveloped in heat. His blood throbbed with radiating life and he was fire itself. His palms pulsed with power. The breath he held inside flamed to a feverish pitch until he exhaled and the fire burst from his hands, spinning in spirals like a dancing dragon.

The flames punished a chanter's head, pouring into his eyes and his body glowed golden orange and steam sizzled from his skin. The chanter screamed in agony. His writhing body issued forth a stream of fire from his mouth, which hungrily ate into the nearby drummer.

The chanter and the drummer melted into ash and only their screams lingered in the forest.

Talis gazed, defiance raging in his eyes. He roared a horrific yell and fire exploded all around him: a multi-fingered fire ripping into village huts and setting them aflame. The fire tendrils issuing from his hands went wild, scorching tree trunks, drummers and chanters alike, until it seemed as if the whole world would turn into a blazing inferno. He felt a terrific agony inside and his bones and tendons buckled under the pressure.

Mara leapt aside as a wave of flame tore in front of her. She looked at him with stunned eyes. Like a rising crescendo, the flames billowed higher: unceasing, unrelenting, and caring little for where they struck. Another flame nearly seared her hair as it ripped past her.

"Talis, stop!" she yelled. He heard her voice, as if from a faraway land, muddled by time, as if a great ocean was in between. Inside his mind, he pictured the fires of the Underworld, a sea of churning red and black embers. More flames leapt out until it seemed as if the air itself would take to flame.

She screamed at Talis. "Enough! You'll kill us all!"

Talis blinked, pulling out of a dark tunnel at the speed of a falcon's dive. He stared at Mara, his senses coming back. What was he doing? He glanced around at the destruction. Had he caused all this? His body still vibrated with the pulse of his charged heart and the heat still fevered inside.

He noticed the movement of his enemies and his determination returned. He wouldn't rest until they were all dead. Wielding his sword, the fire rose again.

One chanter fled into the shadows, searching for consolation. Another drummer threw down her drum, and grabbed a rock and lunged at Talis. He dodged and cut her down. The vial of her body spilled opened and spewed ash. The remaining enemies fled into the darkness.

Fire raged everywhere.

Talis glanced around. His friends had come out of their trances. Mara looked tired, as if she hadn't slept in days. Lenora and Nuella cringed behind Rikar and Nikulo, staring at Talis as if he were some kind of a monster. Lenora's father, the blademaster, and the sorceress were all gone. What had happened to them? The huts blazed and the green fire had gone cold. The burned bones seemed to cry out.

"Where's your father?" Talis said to Lenora.

"They killed him." Tears spilled down her cheeks. "Father is gone, consumed by the fire. Mordellia and Javar tried to stop them...but they were slain and given to the flames."

Talis gazed at the bones and bowed his head. "We have to leave this evil place."

They collected their gear and rounded up their horses. Talis mounted and stared east. A beam of moonlight sliced through the trees. There was still hope. They still had a chance. He rode slowly, but the gloom of the forest stalked him from every shadow.

17

Aurellia

Determined to leave the horror of the village far behind, they rode long and hard that day through the forest, and setup camp along a broad river with burly boulders dotting the beach. A heavy mist blanketed the party in dew. Talis huddled next to the fire, trying to release a chill that had refused to leave his body since casting the fire spell. He glanced over at Lenora, sitting on the other side of the fire, her eyes puffy and red from crying. She was holding her sister tight, shivering, staring into the fire as if she'd seen a monster.

"I'm worried about them," Mara whispered to him.

Talis nodded, and shimmied close to her. "I can't even imagine how they must feel. First they lost a mother and their home, and now this?"

"I know the feeling well," Rikar said, his voice choked and bitter. "It's like having your stomach torn out." He sighed a long time, scraping the ground with his dagger. "When father died I swore I'd get revenge on his enemies—"

"And who might that be?" Talis said, bristling at Rikar's words.

"Start at the top, House Storm." Rikar twirled his dagger. "But fear not, son of House Storm, revenge can wait. Father beckons me from the Underworld."

"The Underworld? Only the dead visit the land of the dead."

Rikar chuckled, as if entertained by some secret joke. "You know little, young Master Storm. There is a way, you know. This was spoken many times in legends of heroes and their adventures far through the world."

"The hero's journey to the Underworld, past the Titans of the deep and the mountain of fire." Mara glanced at him with suspicious eyes.

"This is all true, I've seen it in a vision." Rikar lobbed a stick into the fire. "I've seen my father also...his agony... He's forced to join the Grim March of endless war and resurrection. I *will* rescue him."

"You're going the wrong way." Mara scoffed. "The Underworld is beneath us."

Rikar calmly shook his head. "No, quite the opposite. We're going in exactly the right way. The entrance to the Underworld is on that island."

"How do you know this?" Nikulo said, suddenly alert.

"There are many things that I know that you don't. Enough of this talk. I'm tired." Rikar pulled a wolf skin over himself and turned away to sleep.

The group fell silent. Talis closed his eyes and thought about Rikar's words. The time he'd caught Rikar praying to the shrine of Zagros. His words in the desert. When Rikar had called his master, Aurellia. Who was this Aurellia? Talis was determined to discover the secret...

After everyone was asleep, he glanced at Rikar. He seemed asleep as well, but for some reason Talis could *feel* that he was awake, alert, and waiting. The wind stirred, a moist wind that blew from the east. Rikar shifted slightly, and Talis closed his eyes and observed with his ears. He could hear Rikar rising slowly, creeping from camp.

Seconds later, Talis spotted Rikar stalking along the river. Shadows danced and the moons reflected off the rippling water. Talis followed, trying to stay quiet, and past a bend in the river he glimpsed a dark figure along the shore. Rikar approached the figure and Talis felt a chill run down his spine. He stalked along the forest's edge, trying to get a better view.

Rikar bowed low to the figure. Talis crept even closer, until he could faintly hear what they were saying.

"Obedient boy, you've served me well. Is all according to plan?"

Talis held his breath. The figure was Aurellia, the one who'd saved them from the necromancers in the desert. *Was the sorcerer following them?* Talis thought. In the moonlight, he could see one side of his hideous, wrinkled face beneath a black cape.

"It is." Rikar frowned. "Some complications...but nothing to stand in the way."

"Complications?"

Talis listened to Rikar tell the story of the assault at the huts. Rikar did his best to change the story to paint his own actions (or lack of action) in the best light.

"This friend of yours...Talis Storm. He could prove useful. Could he be swayed in our direction?"

Rikar paused for a moment, as if unsure how to proceed. "Talis has different aims—he longs only to save his city."

"As he should." Aurellia chuckled. The wind changed, gusting up for a moment, and struck Talis's back.

Aurellia stiffened, like a hound catching a scent. He shifted his gaze towards Talis, pits of blackness blazing into the night.

"You were followed...by your friend."

Talis dropped, feeling electricity crawling along his scalp. It was too late to run. Rikar ran over and aimed his fingers at him. Aurellia sauntered over as well, his cloak shuffling along the ground.

"You should have stayed at camp..." Rikar pulled his shoulders back.

"A guest...how quaint. I would have come prepared if I had known I was to receive a guest." Aurellia clasped his hands together, as if trying to solve a puzzle. "Now I could look at this two ways: one, a curious boy, loyal to his friend and concerned for his safety...out here in the wilderness, after all. Or, two, a traitorous boy, spying on a friend and sworn to some foul task. Now which is it?"

Talis stepped out of the shadows and bowed his head to Aurellia. "Curiosity... And I should offer thanks, for saving us in the desert."

"Most polite...impressive. You are quite welcome." Aurellia harrumphed. "A master must protect his loyal apprentices. But enough of history, why are you here now?"

"I should ask the same thing of you and Rikar."

"And insolent. If you wish to preserve the use of your legs, please contain yourself." Aurellia raised a long, crooked finger. "Let's just say, behind the curtain of life, there is a grand struggle. Kingdoms rise and kingdoms fall. Treacherous plans by the rich and the ruthless. Everything you see on the outside is not what it seems."

Rikar grinned. "The master today, is the slave tomorrow—"

"Refrain!" Aurellia glared at Rikar. He paused, then strode close to Talis. "I am old, as old as recorded time…and then a measure more." Talis could smell the sick stench of mold wafting from his wrinkled mouth and wanted to vomit. "Many of this world call me master. You have a choice, young Talis, a choice that will decide your future. You can be patient and assume there is a valid explanation behind this secret meeting, or you can act rashly. The latter would be…a mistake."

A mistake. More like it would cost him his life. He had no choice…

"Apologies for my intrusion." Talis bowed. "I will take my leave." As he walked away, he could hear Aurellia whispering to Rikar.

Before Talis reached the camp, Rikar jogged up to him, breathless.

"Wait…before you—"

"Who is he? Have you been feeding him information all along?" Talis gripped his sword hilt.

Rikar backed away, pressing his palms out. "This conversation is going in the wrong direction. If you try to fight me, you'll lose. That sword will do you no good."

"I want answers…"

"You won't get them from me. Only Aurellia can give you answers, so you'll have to be patient."

"No…you can tell me who he is. How long have you been studying with him?"

Rikar's face contorted to a snarl, glancing down at Talis's fire sword now positioned over his heart. "You really want to do this? You think you can beat me with that sword?"

"I just want answers… You owe me that at least."

"Aurellia is my true master of magic. His knowledge and abilities are beyond any of the wizards of Naru."

"And how did you first find him?"

A pained sigh escaped from Rikar's lips. "After my father was killed, I kept having nightmares of my father tortured in the Underworld. I visited the Temple of Zagros, begging mercy for my father, but the nightmares continued. Once at midnight I bumped into a robed figure worshipping at the Temple. I was surprised, because I'd rarely seen anyone there. I asked the person if he was a temple priest and he chuckled, saying perhaps in a way he was a priest of Zagros.

"The man asked me why I had come here, so I told him my story... It turned out that the man was Aurellia, one of the most powerful magicians in the world. He helped stop the nightmares and once he knew my abilities at magic, he took me in as his apprentice...."

"But who is this Aurellia? Where does he come from?" Talis released his grip and lowered his sword.

Rikar shook his head, his eyes dark and mysterious. "You'll have to ask him that yourself."

"So we go on, continue our quest and act as if nothing has happened?"

"Nothing has happened...yet. Once we get to the island, things will change, I can promise you that. And perhaps you'll have your opportunity to find the answers you seek from Aurellia."

The Surineda Map led them to the island and yet Talis felt like it was a trap waiting to spring. He couldn't trust Rikar, and he didn't feel like he could trust Aurellia, either. But that island was where the map led them and he could feel the power waiting for him, the power of the sun, the power of the Goddess Nacrea.

Talis turned his back on Rikar and stalked back to camp, his mind filled with dark thoughts that refused all his attempts at sleeping. The next morning Lenora glanced at Talis as if she sensed something had changed overnight. Mara noticed also and sent him a look that said, *What's going on?*

He motioned for Mara to follow him over to the river and they sat behind an upturned tree stump.

"You look like you slept in a pile of leaves." Mara brushed a strand of hair from his face.

"I didn't sleep well." He sighed and felt a shudder roll through his body. "After everyone was asleep, Rikar snuck off...to meet the sorcerer who saved us in the desert."

Mara's face paled in disbelief. "The one who slew all the undead?"

Talis lowered his voice and leaned in closer to Mara. "I followed Rikar last night to the river. The sorcerer...Aurellia, he's...he's some kind of a terror. But Rikar told me that he's been studying with him since his father's death."

"Rikar's changed, ever since his father was killed on the hunt."

"Who is this sorcerer?" Lenora said, jumping over the stump, her eyes filled with mischievousness.

Talis bolted upright, startled. "You…you followed us here?"

"This doesn't involve you," Mara said, and brought a dagger out, glaring at Lenora.

Lenora frowned and leaned against the trunk. "It does now, now that my fate is intertwined with yours. I'm not frightened of your pitiful weapons. Now, who is this sorcerer you speak of?"

"We don't need to tell you a thing," Talis said.

"I have ways of finding the truth…gazing into your eyes will tell me more than your lips would ever reveal." Lenora's eyes changed to silver and her pupils widened until they shone bright. Talis felt dizzy, as if he were spinning down into some dark chasm. He pictured Aurellia, slaying the undead in the desert, and Aurellia again, talking with Rikar by the river.

Lenora shrieked, startling Talis awake. He glanced around, spotting Mara straddling Lenora, her daggers pricking the side of Lenora's delicate neck, until a line of blood dripped down.

"Get her off of me!" Lenora shouted, and wriggled under Mara.

"If you continue moving, these pitiful weapons, as you called them, are going to do a lot more damage. Now what were you doing to Talis, you witch… Casting some kind of charm, a truth reveal spell?"

Lenora's body stiffened and a look of triumph crossed her face. "I knew something was strange about your story. People rarely survive attacks from Jiserians… So this sorcerer, Aurellia, is connected with your friend Rikar? And you saw this Aurellia last night? Why is he following us?"

Talis gaped at Lenora in disbelief. How did she know Aurellia's name? Did mystics have the power to read minds? "Talk to Rikar about that… But if you try that trick on me again, you'll wish you hadn't. We'll take you as far as Khael and that's all, you have family there, right?"

Lenora pursed her lips, as if greatly displeased. "You want to get rid of me, don't you?"

Mara let her go and Lenora climbed over the stump and stormed off, her dress swishing back and forth.

"We'll need to watch her," Mara said. "She's a witch. All those tears for her father… Now it's as if she's forgotten about him completely."

"Now she's gone to Rikar… Look, she's talking to him."

"Flirting with him is more like it, and it's working. Why do girls resort to such trickery?" Mara scowled, then blinked as if remembering something. "This morning I woke up and heard Rikar mumbling to himself. It didn't make any sense to me at the time. He said, 'I obey, master, to Darkov... Under the temple, Zagros commands.' What do you think that mean?"

"I've never heard of Darkov, a city perhaps?"

"Look on the map. You can read the runes, right?"

Talis glanced back at the camp, making sure they were all there. He withdrew the map from the case and stretched it out. Immediately the map lit up, symbols and markers glowing as if on fire. All over his body, his skin tingled from holding the map.

"There's Lorello," Mara pointed. "But the island is so small on the map..."

"I wish we could see more detail." As if responding to his desire, the map changed, and now displayed a larger view of the island. New markers appeared. Talis and Mara gasped at once.

"This one says 'Seraka', along the coast."

"And this one, over here?" Mara said, pointing at an area to the south and east where there was an immense marker, and within, a shimmering golden triangle.

"Urgar...and here in the city is the Temple of the Goddess Nacrea, our destination."

"What about this?" She tapped a city to the north, shrouded in mist.

"The City of Darkov..."

18

Intrigue in Khael

After three days of fair weather and hard riding, Talis and the others sat on their horses staring over the City of Khael. The city was nestled in the side of a cleft overlooking the mystical Melovian Sea. The ocean glimmered and glittered as if enchanted by the Goddess Nacrea. Talis had dreamed about seeing the ocean ever since his father had told him bedtime stories of his youth in Onair, of times spent wandering along the beach and sailing in small skiffs on the fair western seas. How he missed his family and his home…

High above the City of Khael, sandstone spires ran along the mountain ridge like a dragon's spine. The sun lingered low over the horizon, painting the countryside in shades of violet and gold. A tower rose from the highest point in Khael, next to the cliffs, part of a palace that shimmered from the last rays of sunlight. He caught sight of a shadow cast from a low cloud that hovered over the harbor, a shadow that sent crooked fingers spidering across the rooftops.

"I don't like how it looks," Mara said. Other than the palace and the surrounding compound, the rest of the city was a dark and dreary hovel. The difference between the two areas was startling. Along the docks and leading up towards the hills, old dilapidated buildings and crumbling earthen homes were crammed in so close together, Talis could hardly spot any streets. He gripped his reins tighter and prodded his horse down the hillside.

As he rode, he noticed that the city was heavily guarded with soldiers marching in many places throughout the city, with a large contingent stationed near the palace. Outside, no guard posts or walls or patrols of any kind protected Khael. It was as if the government had no interest in keeping people out. This struck Talis odd, a stark contrast with Naru's enormous walls and regular patrols.

They reached what appeared to be a town gate: the broken remains of two old stone guardhouses. A man's distended body hung from a guardhouse, a noose cinched around his bulging, purple neck. Where the eyes had once been were now hollow, maggot-strewn sockets, and the rest of him was being torn asunder by a gang of crows eagerly digging and tearing away at his flesh. The stench was so nauseating that Talis covered his mouth and forced himself to look away.

Long shadows knifed their way down the main street past the guardhouse. The narrow streets heard feet stomping away at their arrival. Women from high windows scowled at the party, slamming their shutters closed as they approached, leaving the smell of burned meat and moldy bread to waft into Talis's nostrils.

Past the town square, down spare, winding streets, the way opened up to the docks, and beyond, the Melovian Sea. It went on forever. So this was the sea father had talked about so much. Where you could spend an eternity on those wild waves, drifting from island to island, alongside whales and dolphins and sharks, hoping and praying to reach a friendly port. He could almost feel the rise and lurch of the great ship beneath his feet.

A breeze whipped up and he inhaled, surprised at the smell of fish and other pungent smells he didn't recognize. A sudden craving struck him: to eat the bounty of the sea. He glanced around and hoped to find an inn or a tavern. The docks were teaming with people everywhere, those in uniforms and silk dresses, and throngs of poor in filthy, tattered clothes. Ship's hands, beggars, thieves with shifty eyes, and dotted here and there, soldiers harassing well-dressed sea captains and traders. Ladies of obviously poor-repute sauntered amongst the crowd, looking for victims with coin. Talis spotted an inn called *"The Rusty Harpoon"* and decided it the best choice. Fewer drunks littered the steps outside.

He motioned the others towards the inn and Rikar grunted and guided his horse to the stables, while Lenora's horse trotted next to him.

Mara smirked at Lenora, her eyes filled with contempt. "She's been cuddling up close to him for days."

"Young love." Nikulo flashed his teeth. "Catch me if I start to swoon, more likely I'll spew."

"Our uncle will never approve," Nuella said, and frowned. "I don't know what she's thinking."

"Love's a mystery." Nikulo stuck his finger in his mouth as if pretending to barf.

"She's not in love." Mara scoffed. "She's just using him."

Nikulo laughed appreciatively at that. "Let me say, for the record, Rikar has no problem being used in this particular situation."

Inside the inn was packed and noisy, smelling of smoked fish and ale and garlic. Ladies danced with drunken sailors in uniform, while older officers sat staring, scheming, and drinking. Talis followed Rikar and Lenora to a rickety table in the far corner under the stairs. Chunks of dust tumbled down on them as people stormed up and down.

"No wonder the table was available." Mara waved away the dust.

"It's the only free table...stop complaining," Rikar said, and motioned for a barmaid's attention.

"Always liked a layer of dust with pork roast." Nikulo brushed off the table with his hat.

"Do you have coin?" The barmaid's suspicious eyes studied them.

Rikar flourished a silver coin. "Food and ale...and a room for the night?"

"A room?" Nuella said. "Aren't we to have a room of our own?"

"Aren't you bound for Uncle's house?" Lenora spat, and shifted her chair closer to Rikar's.

"And you aren't?" her sister shot back.

Lenora glanced at Rikar, then shook her head. "I'll not set foot in that drunkard's house."

"But the plan was to live with Uncle and—"

"Plans change, sister. It's hard for me to leave you, but I imagine you'll manage somehow."

The barmaid cast a disapproving glance at them, but swiped the coin from Rikar's hand and stormed off.

"You've scared her." Rikar grinned. "You sisters shouldn't fight. We'll find your uncle tomorrow, and reunite you *both* with your family."

"But you said!"

Rikar put up his hand as if to silence Lenora. "Eat first, your hunger is affecting your mood."

"This seems a good place to ask around for ship's passage to Lorello." Nikulo flicked his eyes towards the seamen at the other tables.

"The crooked lot of them…the whole town included." Rikar narrowed his eyes at an older officer in uniform.

"Be vague then," Talis said. "Ask where they trade, home ports."

Mara sighed. "That's not how it's done. Ask what trade garners the most coin. Pretend like you're interested in signing up as a ship's hand."

The barmaid slapped down a large plate with a haunch of pork, roasted potatoes dripping in oil, and a whole cod—eyeballs included. "Now there's a feast." Nikulo rubbed his hands together and sampled a potato.

"And ale?" Rikar said.

"Save yer fancy mouth for the food." The barmaid huffed. "Ale's coming soon enough. And ya owe another five silver for the room. That foreign coin of yours needs more weight."

Nikulo handed her the coins, and gave Rikar a look as if trying to pacify him. "This is not Naru…prices are different."

"More like local robbery once they saw the foreign mint."

"The *inland* mint… Most people in this room are sailors except for us. Our coin gives us away." Talis noticed the barmaid whispering to the innkeeper.

"We'll see about changing coins in the morning." Nikulo's eyes brightened as the barmaid sauntered up, carrying a tray with six mugs of ale.

"Father complains from the grave," Lenora said, and raised the mug to her lips.

"Your father walks the Grim March in the Underworld." Rikar sneered at her furious eyes. "Begging mercy from Zagros."

Lenora paled and gripped her mug handle so hard that her knuckles went white. A look of utter betrayal raged in her eyes as she glowered at Rikar. But she kept her mouth quiet and raised the ale up to her lips and drank it all in one long gulp.

"You're a cruel bastard," Mara hissed. "Have you truly no feelings at all?"

Rikar slowly shook his head. "Not for many years... I've no need for them. You've enough emotions for the lot of us. Wear them with *royal* Princess pride." He gulped down his ale in one go.

Talis wanted to kill him. He glared at Rikar and seized his sword.

"What do you want? You, the hope of Naru, the young master of noble blood... Do you want to murder me?" Rikar shouted the last part and drew in the bloodthirsty stares from sailors across the room. "You're all just dripping with tender *feelings*. Plump morsels for the Master. Do you all realize how insignificant you are?"

Nikulo coughed. "Indeed we are quite insignificant...next to an ego such as yours. Where are my manners, I forgot to bow down and worship your lordship's arse."

"Go ahead, laugh until your fat face turns red. We'll see how well your wit serves you on that island."

"Promises and threats, my favorite bedtime stories. Is there something you know that we don't know?"

"Volumes, my old friend, volumes." Rikar stood to leave.

"And who pray tell invited you on this quest?" Nikulo looked at Rikar as if puzzled by what he saw. "Am I missing something here? All this talk of Zagros and mystery on the island. We arrive at Khael—a ship's journey away—and *my old friend* shows his true colors?"

Lenora glanced at Talis, as if begging him to say something. Talis cleared his throat. "Rikar here is in league with a dark sorcerer—"

"Say another word and I'll slice your head off." Rikar smiled with madness glittering in his eyes. "I told you he will explain himself when he sees fit. Until then keep those words to yourself."

"Are we to understand that this *master* of yours will explain everything once you lead us to the city of Darkov?" Mara said the last past in a whisper.

"Who told you about Darkov?" Rikar's face paled.

"You did, you stupid fool."

19

Passage to Lorello

Rikar rose early in the morning to escort Lenora and Nuella to their uncle's house, ignoring Lenora's futile final protests. Talis said goodbye to them, noticing the look of trepidation and sadness in Lenora's eyes. He didn't buy her fake emotions for a moment. For some strange reason she wanted to stay with them and continue on to the island, but everyone had agreed they had no interest in having her along.

Talis and Mara went to scour the docks in search of a ship bound for Lorello, and as they left, Nikulo mumbled something about needing to find rare ingredients. *More poison for his potions?* Talis thought. The air was cold and clammy from a dense mist and the ships in the harbor bobbed listlessly, their furled sails disappearing into the fog. A vision flashed in his eyes of those same sails snapping and seizing the wind in a burst of speed. He couldn't wait to go.

"Trade mostly in seal furs from the Isle of Tarasen," an old salty sailor barked in response to Talis's question.

They moved on, trying a broken-down tavern so close to the sea, Talis was sure it would soon fall in.

"Salt…salt from the salt flats of Douraman… We stay close to the coast. Yonder sea is vicious out in the open." The hairy, barrel-chested sailor puffed on a pipe, blowing rings of smoke thoughtfully. "Talk to Captain Calfour. He might know a thing or two about adventure on the high seas. Oldest and craziest dog amongst us."

They tried the Captain and got a sour stare and plenty of grunts. He didn't want their ale and wasn't interested in speaking a word. But as they were leaving the tavern, a man tapped Talis on the shoulder, and motioned them outside and down a dark alley.

"So you're looking to join up on the Captain's ship?" The man wore a crisp white cap, and had two missing front teeth. "I'm his first mate, anything you want to say to the Captain has to go through me."

"And where does your ship sail?" Mara said, her eyes wary of the sailor.

"Quite a lip on this one." The first mate frowned at Mara. "We sail where there's money in the wind."

"Such as?" Talis said, getting frustrated by the vague and colorful answers of the sailors.

"Well if you must know, we sail south to Tsenga, north to Blighter's Bay, and if the need arises, east, far out across the sea...to Seraka."

So there it was, Seraka. Talis hated the look of greed and thievery in the man's eyes, but it was their only lead so far. "And where will you be sailing next?"

The first mate snorted. "The need is great, so we set sail to Seraka at dawn tomorrow. You'll work hard, the wages will be poor and the food awful...but if you've never seen her before, seen the ancient Isle of Lorello, there's gold in that view. Can't ye see her vibrant jungles and flaming mountains and mysterious ruins? Ah, the life of a sailor. I wouldn't trade it for all the salt in the world."

"Then you have room for the four of us?"

"Four?" The man looked puzzled, though in a pleased sort of way.

"Well do you?"

"Of course I'll need to consult— How about I bring the Captain's decision...to your?"

"Inn. The Rusty Harpoon."

"Of course, of course you'd be staying there." The first mate grinned crookedly, and slipped down the alley, disappearing into the shadows.

Nikulo stumbled into their room past midnight, so drunk he hit his head on the bedpost. He bowed and apologized to the bedpost for his clumsiness. Talis found himself chuckling at his stupid inebriation.

"What happened to you?" Mara rubbed her eyes. "And where is Rikar?"

"I last saw my old traitorous friend trying to convince a young maid he was a prince... She didn't believe him."

"He wishes he was a prince."

"That's the funny part." Nikulo staggered around, his eyes gleeful. "How does a boy who looks like a wanton minstrel convince a girl he's trying to bed that he's a prince? "

Mara chuckled. "Rikar can't even sing his own name. Not a minstrel, not a prince, just wanton. By the way, in which tavern did you last see our *old friend*?"

"The Suckling Pig... He was surrounded by new friends with a taste for ale."

"And silver..."

"Nay, always the ale that the silver buys." Nikulo burped, slapping his chest and puffing out his cheeks. "Whew, I'd better lie down."

"Did you ever find those rare ingredients?" Talis said.

Nikulo hiccupped. "Success!" he said, then rolled over and started snoring.

"Shall we go fetch him?" Mara studied Talis, her face disgusted and resigned at the same time.

"I don't see why we should..." Talis wished they could just leave Rikar to fester away here in some shit-hole. Did they really need him along?

The Suckling Pig reeked of vomit and smoke and sweat. It was the filthiest and most crowded tavern Talis had ever seen. There was an enormous round table in the center of the room and Rikar sat at the far end, shaking dice in an ivory cup.

"The gods be pleased, roll sevens!" Rikar shouted. A girl, maybe fifteen, jumped up and down, screeching, not minding her state of undress.

The crowd surrounding the table roared. Sevens... Rikar scooped up a pile of coins, grunted, and destroyed another mug of ale.

"Oy!" Mara shouted. "Time to go, we've found a ship."

Rikar raised his eyes as if annoyed at hearing her voice. "Can't you see I'm winning here?"

"You'll end up losing in the end, whether to the dice or to these...*ladies*." Talis sneered at Rikar. For all his noble upbringing, Rikar showed himself now as the fool he was. First Nikulo and now this. Even if the

Captain let them on as crew, Talis couldn't see how he'd manage to wake everyone up in time.

After Rikar sighed, he shrugged and stuffed the coins into his purse and rose, shaking off the girl who'd clung to his arm. "The night is over...dawn and the sea awaits. Lead on, my prudish friends, may your steps be difficult and the sinkholes you step in rancid." For some reason he laughed to himself, as if caught up in some private joke.

At the door, someone grabbed Talis's arm. He spun around and frowned at the first mate.

"Ye said the Rusty Harpoon... This ain't the place."

"Powers of observation." Rikar scoffed at the man.

"This another of your friends? Tell him to mind his tongue tomorrow morning. Drunk as he is...good luck getting him up. Try a bucket of cold fish, that always does the trick." The first mate tapped his finger on Talis's chest. "First light or we sail without you. Not that the Captain cares, mind you. We sail on the finest ship in the harbor, The Bounty of the Sea. Eighteen canons, seven masts—"

"And a blathering fool that talks too much." Rikar farted and walked past the man, waving the smell in his direction. "I need to water the sea."

Talis chased after Rikar, who shambled his way towards the docks. As Rikar relieved himself into the water, Talis yanked back on his shirt to keep him from falling in. Why he was helping him? Maybe he felt sorry for the fool. Maybe he knew that they'd need him in the days to come. Whatever the reason, Talis and Mara guided Rikar back to the room and shoved him into bed.

The innkeeper woke them before dawn as promised. Nikulo had a long dangle of drool dripping out of his snoring mouth. Rikar was curled into a ball, shivering and mumbling from a bad dream. Talis and Mara stared at them, chuckling. A perfect pair of freakish clowns.

Without time for breakfast, they all headed down to the docks. Nikulo stumbled along, wincing, and pulled his hair as if from a bad headache.

"Never again," he said. "I don't know what that bartender put in those drinks... Something funny going on in his brew."

"With any luck we'll be back again for more." Rikar took a deep breath. "Just what I need, a good sea breeze to keep my spirits up."

"And rolling waves to have you barfing up yesterday's meal." Mara pointed at the seagulls kicking around in the sea. "They'll appreciate it."

"Please don't even mention it," Rikar said slowly, and placed a hand on his stomach. "The world is still spinning."

The first mate ambled up to them, chewing on a fat cigar. "The worst bunch of motley vagabonds I've ever seen. I'm certain you've never even set foot on a ship. Well, you'll learn soon enough. If the food doesn't kill you the sharks likely will. Hey you, fatty, you're looking kind of sick. Is he all right?"

"The sight of your face is making me ill... Apologies for whatever my mouth gushes forth."

"I like him... There's salt in that fatted pork." The sailor grinned a bit too eagerly. "A good choice letting you on after all. Just get on up the gangplank and keep your mouths shut."

Talis stared up at the bow of the largest galley in the bay. A goddess kept watch over her direction, painted in silver and gold and black. Her long flowing golden hair swept down along the sides of the ship, as if the wind might lift her up into the sky. The Bounty of the Sea. Her name made him hungry.

They glanced at each other with uncertain eyes and Talis took the first step and sauntered up the plank, finding the leering eyes of the crew unsettling. Mara jogged up alongside and slid her hand into his, her face fearful and nervous. He squeezed her hand and gave her a reassuring nod. Whatever strange ship they sailed on would have to deal with them as a group, for in the fierce, determined eyes of Rikar and Nikulo he found companions he felt he could trust in a fight. As long as Talis could keep Rikar on his side.

"Make yerself at home," a midget of a sailor shouted, and gestured towards the rail as they reached the deck.

A deep, droning horn sounded, announcing their departure to the still sleepy city. The crew raised the gangplank and cranked the anchor in. At the docks, a horde of cats ran by, as if expecting a fresh new load from the sea. The galley shuddered as the sails popped, taking ahold of a cold, morning breeze. Soon they were out past the docks and navigating through the winding harbor and out into the vast, blue sea.

For the first time since their journey started, Talis felt hope surging inside his heart. They'd finally found a ship to the island of their destination. The Surineda Map had been true, the words of the hero true. Out on that island lay the promise of a power so strong, they might actually have a chance of saving their city.

If they could survive the dark journey ahead.

33903334R00145

Made in the USA
Lexington, KY
15 July 2014